MW01016153

Shonagh Koea was awarded the Fellowship in Literature at the University of Auckland in 1993 and the Buddle Findlay-Sargeson Fellowship in Literature in 1997. She was a finalist in the 1995 New Zealand Book Awards with *Sing To Me, Dreamer*, her third novel. Her fifth novel, *The Lonely Margins of the Sea* was runner-up for the Deutz Medal for Fiction in the Montana Book Awards in 1999. Shonagh Koea has given lectures and readings at the International Festival of the Arts in Wellington, the Canberra World Festival, the Listener Women's Book Festival and for the New Zealand Book Council.

the WOMEN'S
BOOKSHOP
105 Ponsonby Rd
Auckland, N.Z.
Ph: 0-9-376 4399

TIME FOR A KILLING

SHONAGH KOEA

VINTAGE

A VINTAGE BOOK
published by
Random House New Zealand
18 Poland Road, Glenfield, Auckland, New Zealand
www.randomhouse.co.nz

First published 2001

© 2001 Shonagh Koea

The moral rights of the author have been asserted

ISBN 1 86941 465 9

Cover design and illustration: Julie Davis
Printed in Malaysia

The author gratefully acknowledges Creative New Zealand for a publishing grant to assist with the writing of this work.

CHAPTER
ONE

The ghosts at 10 Fleming Street — Claude, Frederick, Florence and Eduardo — were all sitting on the stairs, in various attitudes of despondency, as evening fell on the fifth of February last year. Below them, in the entrance hall, the only piece of furniture was a treacle-varnished sideboard of no distinction on which rested a small pressed glass vase containing four bilious yellow daisies, four sprigs of fern and four zinnia blooms ranging in colour from deepest puce to wild orange.

'Moira's taste is all in her mouth,' Florence would sometimes say sadly. Moira and Kevin Crumlatch had owned the house for the past decade. The vase stood on an imitation crocheted doily made of beige plastic with a dull finish to simulate genuine écru thread. Florence also regarded this sadly and her concentration was such that she was sometimes able to make the hall light flicker a little on evenings when electrical storms might be imminent. The weather this particular evening was balmy with a reasonably showy and cheerful sunset over the sea which was about half a mile away at the end of a steeply wooded valley. The house at 10 Fleming Street stood at the head of the valley, on a promontory. The atmosphere on the stairs, though, was one of unmitigated gloom. Florence sat with her head in her hands. She was the one who had first commented on the Crumlatchs' taste the day they moved in. Claude had just said, 'Are they on the Planet Earth or not, man?' when all their 1960s furniture with pokey-out legs was carried in. Then he had made theatrical vomiting noises.

7

Eduardo was slumped now against the panelled wall of the stairwell with his eyes closed as if he had fallen into a restless sleep. His hands twitched faintly. Claude sprawled at the foot of the stairs whittling away at his left index finger with the spectre of a penknife he had been given when he was nine. He had been a ghost much longer than any of the others and was more widely experienced in spectral behaviour, and also in chemistry because he had been training as a pharmacist when he cut his finger and died of septicaemia at the age of twenty-two. Florence was his sister, although she looked more like his grandmother because she had lived to eighty-three.

'I do wish you wouldn't do that, Claude,' she whispered. 'I've told you before — it really makes me feel quite ill.' They all spoke very quietly before midnight but after that they sometimes made quite a bit of noise. Claude even sang occasionally about one in the morning and made howling noises out the upstairs windows to start off the odd cat fight or make the dogs bark in the neighbourhood. Eduardo often picked out the odd series of little notes on the Crumlatchs' highly polished upright piano so Frederick could tune one of his violins and Kevin Crumlatch, rolling around in the orange polyester sheets on the master suite's king-size bed, would say, 'Jeez bloody Wayne, the wind makes a helluva row round this old house, Moira, I'll have to do something about it one of these days,' before ejaculating immediately after only just achieving penetration. Moira endured all this without a murmur and mostly thought about what she was going to do tomorrow when he had gone down to the shop, or sometimes she thought about her shopping list — an idea that she found most soothing. Marmalade, tinned peaches, bath cleaner, toothpaste, bread. It made the time pass more quickly.

The Crumlatchs owned a shop in town and from it they had made a fortune. Kevin was planning an early retirement and had had the shop on the market for a few weeks. A sale seemed imminent. The ghosts were a little uncertain about what the Crumlatchs sold but Frederick said that it must be trash that broke during the first week of usage to cause such constant sales. Florence thought it might be vacuum cleaners because she had been an immaculate housekeeper in her day and had always succumbed to the blandishments of a new vacuum cleaner. Claude thought it was definitely fast cars. Eduardo had made no authoritative statement as yet but they expected one any day now. Claude, meanwhile, said that he thought Eduardo was going to claim the Crumlatchs sold electronic equipment of the worst sort, perhaps personal computers with luminous blue screens and matching swivel chairs, or similar items. 'Claude, dear — do, please stop that.' Florence was still watching her brother sharpen his finger. 'I know it's just a little mannerism you've got and you don't mean any harm, but it does make me feel funny.'

'Sorry.' Claude began to gather up the pieces. He was devoted to his sister and she adored Claude. When he died she and Frederick, her husband, had closed up his bedroom and it had remained almost undisturbed till Frederick died decades later. 'But what does it matter?' Claude muttered, continuing to gather up the shreddings. He put them back on his finger where they fell into place immediately.

From the head of the stairs, around the second bend, came a deep rumbling cough. Frederick, Claude's brother-in-law, was about to speak. They all sat up.

'I really do not think,' said Frederick from his unassailable position on the highest stair, 'that I can stand it a moment longer.' It was unlike Frederick to speak so loudly at that hour of the day. A sign of desperation perhaps, Florence thought. Frederick, at ninety-five, was the oldest. He had outlived both Claude and Florence but they had given him the most senior position at the head of the stairs by tacit understanding when, spectrally speaking, he had arrived back in their midst. His final sojourn in a hospital for the very elderly had been mercifully brief — only eight days and all of them in a coma, one of his longest ever absences from home. He and Florence had seldom gone away on holiday as they grew older and after she died he just remained there, pottering away in the garden and moving in smaller and smaller circles till, at last, he stopped altogether. He had been found lying semi-conscious at the foot of the stairs by a neighbour.

Eduardo was the most recent ghost but they all got on extremely well because they were either fondly related or had had the greatest regard for each other in real life. They were also architecturally united because they had all lived in the old house at some time or another and had been very happy there. Florence had said that it would be unseemly for her favourite brother to rent a bedsitter or a flat, even if a suitable one had been available, when she and Frederick owned such a large house. 'Who else would you live with, dear heart,' she had said to Claude then, 'when you need a home?' Their parents had died the previous year within months of each other and, as Frederick sometimes remarked at the time, this suddenly made Florence and Claude adult orphans and Claude virtually homeless after a family farm had to be sold.

Eduardo had purchased the house from Frederick's trustees and had planned to live in it till he, too, was ninety-five. He had known Frederick quite well when he, Eduardo, was a young man starting out in life and Frederick had been more than middle-aged. They had been neighbours then and Frederick had advised Eduardo about gardening and had given him seed potatoes of rare old breeds. He had told him how to grow vigorously sweet and hugely plump rhubarb of no acidity and how to prune roses back to the best outward bud. Eduardo's father had been an unsatisfactorily stupid man who drank too much, ate a lot and constantly burbled an unpalatable and enormous stream of valueless words so when Eduardo became Frederick and Florence's neighbour he secretly adopted Frederick.

At the time, Eduardo had just bought a very small bungalow simply because it was the only house he could afford and that the bank would lend him money on. Part of its garden, right down at the bottom right-hand corner, abutted the big property that Frederick and Florence owned and now haunted, and that is how Frederick and Eduardo met. They used to talk to each other through the hedge when they were working in their respective vegetable gardens, many of the plants in Eduardo's given to him by Frederick. After Frederick died Eduardo had bought the old house. He had been able to do this simply because nuances in the real estate market had greatly inflated the value of the bungalow he and Lydia owned so they sold it very profitably. The interest rate for his new, large and worrisome mortgage was low, though he had not had to worry unduly about repaying it because he had had a heart attack and died at fifty-eight and so the mortgage was repaid by his mortgage repayment insurance. Thus Lydia had wept bitterly for Eduardo in a house suddenly unencumbered by any debt. Eduardo had planned to breed rhododrendrons on the property. The garden was big enough to do anything in, even play football if you wanted to. The first new rhododendron was to be called after Frederick and the second after Florence as a mark of respect, but none of this had come about because Eduardo had died after living in the old house for only three years. His wife Lydia had also known Frederick and Florence very well and Florence had taught her how to make a particularly specialised form of relish for cold meats out of rhubarb and red onions.

Eduardo suffered from fits of depression now because the suddenness of his death had shocked him beyond belief but Claude had been a great help to him. Sometimes they would both sit on the bottom stair, whittling away at their left index fingers while Florence sighed and Claude would say things like, 'Look, buddy boy, if anyone knows where you're coming from on this I do because look at me, man — I snuffed it when I was only twenty-two and I hadn't even had a girl. How do you think that makes me feel?' (Claude sometimes watched the Crumlatchs' television and had picked up a garbled version of the jargon of varying eras.) 'At least you were married and had Lydia and all that stuff. I suppose a cute little blonde like that would have been good — well, you know, wouldn't she? You'd know all about ninety-nine and all that,' he would say wistfully.

'Sixty-nine,' Eduardo used to sigh. Claude never got it right.

'What?'

'Never mind,' said Eduardo.

'Listen.' That was Frederick again. 'I just can't take it any more.'

Yet another Crumlatch row was erupting in the kitchen. Claude crept forward and listened at the closed door. 'Poor old Moira's crying,' he said. 'She doesn't want to sell the house and he says they've got to.'

From the kitchen came Kevin's thunderous voice. 'It's time to make a killing.' He was shouting now and thumping the table to emphasise every word. 'That's what we bought the place for and that's what we're going to do. We're definitely putting the house on the market, Moira, and we're going to make a mint with all my improvements — the en suite, all my crazy paving, the new kitchen, you name it. That's why we came here and that's what we're going to do.' The sobbing became louder.

'For heaven's sake, Moira, pull yourself together.' Kevin Crumlatch stood for a few moments in the old entrance hall after slamming the kitchen door behind him. 'Anyone would think,' he shouted, 'that you don't want to tour the entire country with me for a whole year in our very own mini-bus. How else am I going to mark my official retirement from the world of commerce?'

The kitchen itself was now completely quiet. Frederick put on his spectral spectacles to look through the wall and said Moira was sitting at the kitchen table with her head in her hands, still crying but making no noise.

'They're both so awful,' said Florence, 'but I think he's much worse than she is. She does at least try. There's that flower arrangement she always does in the hall, for instance.'

12

Eduardo groaned.

'I know exactly what you mean, Eddie,' she said, 'but you must give credit where credit's due, and she does try.' She got out a ball of rose pink wool from the pocket of her coat and began to cast on another piece of knitting. She always kept her favourite knitting needles mysteriously stowed away in her tiny evening bag and, in moments of crisis, she would begin knitting her favourite cardigan again, the one she had had back in 1929.

They were all wearing their favourite clothes, as did most of the ghosts in the street, except for Mrs Huddlestone from the little green house down the road who wore her apron. But she had her black bike with her still and that, as Claude said, gave her a real edge over them all. None of them had a bike, although Frederick claimed that his 1937 Chevrolet was still in the garage superimposed over Kevin Crumlatch's Subaru. Florence was wearing her best grey coat with the roll collar in genuine cashmere and a pair of navy blue court shoes with an ornamental cut-out pattern across the top. She usually had her best navy blue hand-embroidered evening bag tucked under her arm ready to go out with Frederick, except they always stayed home now. Frederick wore his dinner jacket. He had been a noted violinist and, in his heyday, went out a lot in the evening to play in chamber music quartets and in various concerts where he was first violin in an orchestra. Some of the happiest moments of his life had occurred when he was in evening dress with his beloved Florence in the front row of the circle ready to applaud at the end of the final movement of something by Beethoven. Beethoven was Frederick's favourite and he lived in hopes that one day they might be able to make contact with the great man and get him to visit.

Claude usually wore his laboratory coat and Eduardo had adopted olive green corduroys with a soft beige woollen shirt and brown suede desert boots as his eternal costume. Sometimes he also wore a Harris tweed sports jacket with leather buttons and leather patches on the elbows. He had

13

been an accountant and mostly wore a suit to his office but had been happiest when he was working in his garden in his corduroys or walking in the park with Lydia — in another slightly less shabby pair of corduroys and his old Harris tweed jacket. Lydia would wear green velvet jeans with Spanish riding boots and a mink blazer.

Sometimes, particularly in the summer when the evenings were long, Eduardo, Florence and Claude talked about going out driving in the Chevrolet.

'Maybe just a breath of fresh air would do us good,' Florence would say wistfully, looking almost fervently out the old stairwell window. This the Crumlatchs had not altered yet although Kevin Crumlatch was threatening to bring the glazier in any day now to replace the rose-coloured glass.

'What colour do you want then?' Moira Crumlatch's voice had contained, they thought, a peculiar savagery.

'Yellow.'

'I'm not having yellow.'

'Yellow's a good colour.'

'Yellow's the colour of calf shit.'

'I'm shocked at you, Moira. I never thought I'd hear you talk like that.'

'I'm shocked at you, Kevin. If you take that pink glass out of that window I'm leaving.'

'Leaving? Leaving, Moira? Am I hearing you right? If I have the pink glass replaced with yellow you're leaving, as in l-e-a-v-i-n-g? Moira, don't put a gun in my hands like this — it may be too tempting.'

The cranberry glass in the stairwell leadlight window remained, though. They noticed that. There was no further mention of yellow.

Years ago when Frederick and Florence were alive, before Florence grew too frail to go out, they had always gone to town in the Chevrolet on a Tuesday. On Mondays Florence made out her shopping list and planned what she was going to wear on the excursion. Frederick got the car out and polished it up a bit and checked the oil and water. They had had it since new but by the time Florence died the old Chevrolet had become almost a sight on the road. People stopped and stared as it went by at exactly 9.35 a.m., Florence sitting up in the front seat, wearing a hat and holding her handbag with daintily gloved little hands, Frederick clutching the wheel firmly and driving steadfastly down to the main street.

Mrs Huddlestone, who had helped them in the house for forty years, remained at home wandering about with the vacuum cleaner, polishing windows, dusting the blinds and getting a cooked lunch ready for twelve thirty sharp when the tyres of the Chevy would crunch on the gravel drive and Frederick and Florence would be home again for another week. Then Mrs Huddlestone would bike home, still wearing her apron. A year or so after Florence died Frederick failed his driving test owing to poor eyesight but this made little impression on him because he had no heart to go to town any more. Mrs Huddlestone did odd bits of shopping for him after that and Florence had left so many preserves in the kitchen cupboards it took him a long time to eat them. His needs and wants decreased dramatically, so not being able to drive the old Chevrolet any more hardly impinged upon his consciousness.

He did not know then that Florence sat on the stairs and watched him sadly and often said to Claude, 'Oh poor Frederick — he did love the car, you know, Claude. He did love to drive the car.' She would begin to cast on the pink knitting again. 'I do really think they could have let him keep his licence. It wasn't as if he went anywhere much, just straight down the road to the main street, Claude. The car knew its way. They could have let Frederick just sit there behind the wheel. He wasn't doing any harm.' But the car, now, sometimes came into their thoughts and they would discuss it gently when they sat on the stairs to watch the sun go down.

'I don't see why,' Claude would say, 'we can't go out in the car now we're all ghosts. I'd like to go to the beach. I might be able to find a surfboard that someone left behind, even if it didn't have an ankle strap, and I could go surfing. I've never been surfing.'

'What about sharks?' Frederick looked up from the financial pages of yesterday's newspaper which Kevin Crumlatch had left on the stairs by accident. Frederick loved to read the newspaper if someone left it lying about near the stairs. He particularly favoured news about shares and theatrical reviews with an emphasis on music.

'If there were any sharks they couldn't eat me because I'm a ghost.' Claude's logic could not be faulted. 'And they'd be ghosts so their teeth couldn't bite properly. Real sharks couldn't see me, only ghosts of sharks.'

'We'll think about it.' Frederick continued to read the paper.

'But you always say that,' said Claude. 'You've been thinking about it for years and in the meantime I've been waiting and waiting to go surfing and go to coffee bars and milk bars and the cinema and everywhere.'

'I've lost my licence.' Frederick spoke with genuine regret. 'I feel very badly about it, Claude my boy, I do really. If I could take you surfing and around all the restaurants and places you want to go I'd gladly drive you, Claude, but I can't break the law. I can't drive the car because I haven't got a licence.'

Claude sighed. 'I've never even been to a record store to buy an Elvis Presley LP,' he said, 'and now he's been dead for years and I never will now. I'm just trying to have a life.'

'I know, dear.' Florence patted his hand. 'But there's another thing about going out in the car that we have to consider. There's that police patrol nearly outside our gate sometimes now — I've seen it from upstairs — and they've got all that electronic equipment particularly on a Friday and Saturday night. How would we know, if we did go out in the car, that somehow we wouldn't be picked up on their sensors. It could be very embarrassing,' said Florence, 'explaining who we are, and you know how possessive and protective Mrs Huddlestone is. The moment she heard we'd been caught down the road driving without a licence and in a peculiar state she'd be off down Fleming Street on her bike to rescue us and heaven knows what would happen.'

'Maybe we better all stay at home then,' said Claude. He sighed regretfully.

'That's right, dear.' Florence patted his knee. 'You just wait till midnight and start making all the dogs bark and a few things like that. You can have lots and lots of fun at home.'

Eduardo stirred a little. He had seemed to be sunk in a reverie all day. 'I used to be a champion swimmer,' he said. 'If you like, Claude, I could show you some photographs of swimming carnivals and I could let you see my trophies. I've got pictures of the surf life-saving champs going right back.' There were a couple of loose floorboards in the smallest bedroom upstairs that Frederick, years ago, had had as a hiding place for money and valuables and which they now all used as a place to secrete the few remnants of their past lives. Eduardo kept his photograph albums there and also a beautiful and very small picture in an ivory frame of himself and the lovely Lydia on their wedding day.

'You two boys go and look at the pictures, then,' said Florence. She always called Claude and Eduardo you two boys. 'And I'll try to think of a treat to brighten everyone up. Perhaps we could make the lights go on and off.'

'I prefer making his bathwater go freezing cold without warning,' said Frederick. He possessed a deep-seated loathing for Kevin Crumlatch.

'I'd rather have a turn with the spectacles and see through walls,' said Claude.

'We'll do them all.' Florence, this evening, was behaving recklessly and uncharacteristically. 'Let's live a little.'

CHAPTER TWO

M eanwhile in the metropolis, many kilometres to the north, things were beginning to hot up for the evening at the Côte d'Azur. The establishment was set deep in the city's red light district, close to the waterfront so it could service cruise ships, ordinary vessels, larger yachts that moored in the viaduct basin, and was only a block or two away from the High Court and the high-rise buildings that housed the more vigorous types of lawyer and businessman who liked to cavort lasciviously rather than going home in the evening to wives of excessive dullness who didn't want their hair mussed up.

The building itself was a prime piece of real estate on three floors, all of them freehold and in good physical and decorative order with a splendid roof made from antique tiles flown especially from Sicily where Richard Villetto, the owner, had gangster connections. Mr Villetto regularly had the exterior painted and sealed and the latest colours used were a discreet kind of ochre on the stone walls with the window frames lacquered French green. The effect was very chic. All the massage parlours had a gimmick and Richard Villetto's public relations consultant had persuaded him that the wholegrain, healthy approach would lead to happy customers and much money in the till. Before and after their activities, to enhance and then restore their blood sugar levels, all the customers were given cocktail sandwiches made from wheatgerm bread with some kind of reasonably fashionable and expensive filling. Smoked salmon always went down well, particularly if it was coupled with some diet cream cheese, and a lot of the customers liked sliced gherkin on a bed of low-fat cottage cheese with a few drops of pure lemon juice, freshly squeezed, and a sprinkling of freshly ground black pepper.

The Côte d'Azur had chairs and sofas that were re-upholstered at least once a year in handwoven fabrics made by genuine peasants in Peru. The resident doctor, who spoke three languages fluently, had received his main qualifications at the Sorbonne. It was one of the very best establishments on the red light district's main drag and, as evening fell, Richard Villetto often stood outside its quaintly wrought portico, made to a special commission by one of the country's leading metal sculptors, with a certain sense of satisfaction about his business and his life.

At home his beautiful wife Ambrosia would be singing, somewhat badly, excerpts from opera as she put their children to bed with the help of the live-in nanny. The children themselves were extremely musical, well behaved and promising in every way. Sebastiano played the flute excellently for a child of only seven and showed a definite promise of good looks. Annunciata, budding slightly at eleven, sang much better than her mother, which was not to say she sang at all well, but her radiant good looks were such that notes slightly off key and the odd quavering warble could be discounted. Richard Villetto hoped she would marry very well, perhaps a lawyer like the ones who frequented his establishment or a High Court judge or just anyone who earned a lot and was what Mr Villetto called well placed. Even earning a lot and not being so very well placed would do, he sometimes thought as he listened to his daughter singing.

Inside the Côte d'Azur Mrs Geraldine Jackson was out in the recently redecorated French Provincial-style kitchen making the sandwiches for the evening's customers. She had concocted a special plate full of small Marmite and lettuce sandwiches for Mr Somerset-Smith's night because, being a regular, his wishes and wants were known very well by the kitchen staff. Mr Somerset-Smith was one of their very oldest and most revered customers and his advanced age made him, sociologically speaking, immune to any fashions in food. Mr Villetto liked the place to be like a home where a business-man, weary after a hard day, could relax and have exactly what he wanted. Mr Somerset-Smith was eighty-two and he seldom actually accomplished anything much these days but he still liked to come in for one evening a week and talk over old times with the girls and particularly with Mrs Jackson, whom he had known since she was only forty-seven.

Oswald, the doorman, was hunting around in the big store cupboard off the back hall for a large and ornamental twig broom. He liked to stand picturesquely under the front portico as the customers began to arrive each evening and be seen to be sweeping in a wholesome homespun manner with the handmade broom imported especially from Provence. Mrs Jackson had been one of Mr Villetto's first employees years ago when he had just a small establishment above a takeaway bar, long before the stockmarket crash and before the tastes of the customers became so rarefied. She had been a winning blonde woman then and she had done all the usual things. Frontwards, backwards, sideways — that type of thing. Nothing fancy. The punters had been well satisfied. It was long before *A Clockwork Orange* became a cult movie and gave customers ideas, and before all the court cases and press releases about the habits of overseas politicians and pop singers gave them more finely honed opinions about what they wanted in the way of fun.

In those days none of the girls wore black leather and no one had a whip or a stick or anything extra. In those days being locked in a cupboard was just called being locked in a cupboard and if you were hung by the neck till you were dead, or even only half dead, it was done in jail for murder. The very idea of having whips polished at twilight and sticks sharpened and black leathers done with nugget and special cupboards full of sharp nails to lock people in to be faintly punctured before they wrote out large cheques in payment —

well, Richard Villetto, in those days, would have shrugged and said you were mad. Now he shrugged and said that he and his business had to move with the times and he went ring-a-ding-ding on the till, smiling broadly.

Geraldine Jackson was now nearly seventy and had retired but Mr Villetto had kept her on to make sandwiches and look after the girls like a mother. She taught them various physical exercises to preserve their inner thighs from pressure and strain, and other tricks to make the customers hurry up if they were taking too long. Mrs Jackson had taught them, as a final resort, to whisper, murmur or shout, 'Hurry up, darling — I've got another punter in five minutes.' Mr Villetto liked reading books about the great country houses and castles of England and he had latched onto the idea of the old family retainer. He thought of Mrs Jackson as just such a person and, out of loyalty to her long and faithful service, had told her she could have a job forever at the Côte d'Azur and also a place to live for her lifetime. She had a little bedsitter up at the top of the building, under the eaves, and with a small balcony looking out over the sea. On this she grew geraniums of the better sort and sometimes just one cyclamen, always white because purity fascinated her.

Oswald had also been part of Mr Villetto's early history in vice. He was now seventy-five but had been a real stud in his day. He walked with a limp because he had wrenched the main cartilage in his left knee so many times as the women shouted 'More! More!' He also had a bedsitter up under the eaves but, on his days off, he mostly stayed around the place tying more picturesque twigs on the broom and reading Mr Villetto's books about the stately homes of England. He did not move out much these days.

Mrs Jackson always went to a department store round the corner on her days off, except if they fell on a Sunday, to have lunch in the cafeteria and do the odd bit of shopping. She got ideas for sandwich fillings there, too. Her needs and wants were very small — an occasional little bottle of Chanel No. 5

took her fancy and perhaps some of the better moisturisers which she smoothed on her lizard-like extremities while thinking of the old days and how her fine pale heels had bruised many backs. She used to think it would be nice if Oswald went with her on these shopping expeditions but he said it would be too embarrassing with rich elderly ladies, even after all these years, recognising him and coming up to clutch his arm and talk wildly about old times. So Oswald mostly just stayed home in the Côte d'Azur, vacuuming any dust out of the handwoven upholstery and tending the many rare cycads and aloes Mr Villetto grew extensively in the bondage room. The air there was warm and damp, and the plants just loved it.

Mr Villetto's children came to visit once a year, right on Christmas after the festive tree had been put up in the foyer, and the families of all the staff also came in for a bit of a do and to get their presents from a hired Santa. Annunciata and Sebastiano called Mrs Jackson and Oswald Nana and Granddad because their actual grandparents were far way in Sicily and the children hankered faintly for family ties. Both the real grandfathers had been shot years before in gangland warfare, but had recovered to lead lives of diminished prowess in all fields except making money. The gifts they sent for the children were truly stupendous: matching teddybears made of mink and with diamond collars, and a genuine cloth-of-gold apron with a diamond-studded halterneck for Ambrosia to wear when she went out to the kitchen to tell the caterers to hurry up with dinner.

Mrs Jackson sometimes went to Annunciata's dancing recitals, and Annunciata would say to her teacher, 'This is my Nana,' which indeed Mrs Jackson was, in her heart, because she loved the little girl and had no family of her own. When Sebastiano played cricket for his school he always wanted Mrs Jackson to be there, sitting in a deckchair under the trees with all the other grandmothers and he would fetch her a cup of tea from the tea tent. 'Here's your tea, Nan,' he would say.

She had photographs of all these occasions on the small mantelpiece in her bedsitter and she kept them in silver frames as, she imagined, a proper family retainer would do. Ambrosia Villetto liked reading books about notable beauties in history and society, her particular favourite being Jacqueline Kennedy Onassis. When she read that Jacqueline Kennedy's grandchildren called her GrandJackie she also gave this name to Mrs Jackson so when they were all at a school cricket match the little family group whose livelihood stemmed from the Côte d'Azur had a curious cachet, a style, that many others lacked. Mrs Jackson would wear her best guipure lace blouse buttoned right up to the neck and fastened with a cameo and would behave beautifully, just like a real grandmother should, but some, she noted with interest, did not. There was sometimes the odd slightly inebriated grandmother teetering by the drinks tent and being hustled away by a daughter-in-law, a flushed son loitering sadly by a car with the passenger door open. That was not Geraldine Jackson's way. Her behaviour was always exquisitely beautiful and reliable, and the Villetto family loved her.

'Are you all right, darlink? GrandJackie?' Ambrosia would ask during these afternoons, her accent slightly thickened for effect or if she had been watching old Ingrid Bergman movies.

'I'm just fine, thank you, dear.' That would be Mrs Jackson at her most gracious and grandmotherly. They all did it so well anyone would have thought it was real. There were, though, occasional faintly embarrassing moments. A few times — perhaps even more than that — a grandfather or two had stopped to raise his panama hat to Mrs Jackson as she sat in her deckchair accidentally displaying her still very lovely legs which, in their day, had been a byword — 700 centimetres of true bliss.

'I feel sure we must have met somewhere.' This is the sort of thing that would be said. 'How do you do? You look so very familiar I'm sure I should know who you are, yet I can't just place —' The voices would fade away then. And Mrs

Jackson would tell them she was just there to watch her little grandson play cricket.

'That's him out there,' she would say, 'the sweet little boy just on the left almost behind the big tree.' They would point out their own grandsons to her, and off they would go to the tea tent, faintly puzzled, perhaps entirely forgetting the original purpose of the conversation and yet deeply satisfied by the faint echo of distant promise they had inadvertently recalled just for a moment or two. Mrs Jackson remembered them all. One had been a High Court judge with very red hair and a very dull wife. Another had been just an ordinary lawyer, so reticent in ordinary life that he merely did conveyancing and left the court work to juniors, and yet his behaviour in private had been so bold, so very unshy that Mrs Jackson sat laughing under the flowering cherry trees when he had limped away. He had become grey now and had told her about his hip replacements, as one will often tell a stranger of illnesses that are taboo in ordinary company.

'Well, I must away,' he said to her jollily and raised his walking stick in salute. 'Shame I can't remember where we met but I'm sure I do know you from somewhere a long time ago. Happy days,' he shouted. 'Happy days.' But Mrs Jackson was always sanguine in her temperament and these incidents did not bother her very much. Even if the old men had recalled exactly where and how they had known her she was equally certain they would also remember that she had been beautiful and kind and this, in her old age, she would not have minded.

On the evening of the fifth of February things were beginning to jump slightly at the Côte d'Azur. Mrs Jackson had made this nice tray of lettuce and Marmite sandwiches for Mr Somerset-Smith and Alice, one of the younger girls, had found the Voltaren in case his knees locked. Two other reliably lovely and active girls had arrived ready for their night's work and bookings, though steady, were not so heavy that Mr Villetto thought he would be in any kind of trouble with a

24

lighter than usual staff. There were no cruise ships in port so he had decided they could all have a dummy run with the new costumes to see what reaction they provoked.

The costumes had prompted a lot of comment and interest in the establishment for several weeks. Since the Entertainers' Collective had assumed considerable union power in the area Richard Villetto was unable just to decide on new costumes and have them made up without consulting the girls. So the process of getting new clothes — or non-clothes — for Alice, who was a novice but coming along well, and all the rest of them had taken several months of negotiation. Lydia, his chief girl, was better versed in business than most of the others because she had once been married, so she claimed, to an accountant who specialised in industrial commerce. She had been very inconveniently articulate about what type of costume would be best and also legal for them all. Mr Villetto had found it all very tiring. Lydia was one of his best girls and he was very fond of her because she brought good business to the building and had a raft of regulars who paid extremely well. But he sometimes rather regretted her sad history because, he thought, it had made her aware of such things as the rights of the individual.

She had come to him on the recommendation of a taxi driver who had been deeply impressed by her behaviour when a well-known stockbroker had attempted to violate her on the back seat of the cab one winter's night several years ago. The driver sometimes drove in bank heists organised by one of Mr Villetto's gangster second cousins, so word got about among the riff-raff and molls that here was a lady who knew how to act. She had grabbed the broker's balls and twisted them till he ordered the driver to go to the nearest hole in the wall where he withdrew six thousand dollars in cash which he gave to Lydia. After that she hit him under the nose with the side of her left hand while extracting his wallet with the other, took his diamond-studded Rolex watch and his antique signet ring set with a rare eighteenth-century

25

intaglio, climbed into the taxi again and gave the order to drive on over both his ankles.

'You got to have her, boss,' said the driver next day when he told the story to Mr Villetto who was always on the lookout for girls of suitable violence and good looks. 'That's some dame. I got her address.' He handed over a piece of crumpled paper.

Lydia had been an ornament to the establishment, Mr Villetto knew, but her previous life sometimes intruded into the even tenor of the Côte d'Azur. For instance, when he had mentioned cut-outs being part of the new costumes Lydia had insisted the doctor must be consulted re the size that was medically judicious and had got the girls to vote on it. There had been weekly meetings at which he showed the staff various preliminary drawings of garments and a clothes designer from one of the best suburbs had been brought in to speak to each girl and find out exactly what she needed and wanted. They had all, separately, reached a decision that cut-outs were a necessity and that black leather was a cliché, as were silver studs. If they all had their ears pierced in four places and their navels in two, with a possible diamond stud also in the navel, that was all the metal and extra material that was necessary.

The fifth of February was the first night the costumes were to be worn, and excitement was running high. The clothes designer had brought the clothes to the building in his own delivery van, the usual driver having suddenly been given the evening off. Even though it was dark the designer wore Giorgio Armani sunglasses, black Italian loafers, black Versace jeans and a black crewneck pullover in woven silk. He looked like an extremely successful burglar. Each ensemble, slightly different, was packed in a large heavy cardboard dress box and, within that, wrapped tenderly in tissue paper in natural earth colours. There were, sadly, no labels on the boxes, no printed logos on any of the paper, and no maker's labels sewn on these garments because it had been a part of the contract that the designer wished to remain completely anonymous, while receiving the large fee associated with the work. After much discussion, chamois leather had been decided on. 'Black leather creaks,' nagged Alice yet again during one of the regular staff meetings and several of the girls actually raised their voices and shouted, 'Hear, hear.'

'And the tight pants get knees in them when you bend over or kneel.' Celine also raised her voice in a way Mr Villetto thought was unbecoming. They were usually very quiet and had been trained by Mrs Jackson to speak in only the sweetest and most beguiling of whispers except for when they had to have a turn with Mr Somerset-Smith who was so deaf they all had to shout, or if they had to finally tell people to hurry up. Usually Lydia did Mr Somerset-Smith because she was very good with the elderly and if he fell asleep as she was undressing him she just calmly took off the rest of his clothes and left him slumbering on a cream satin bed under a lightly embroidered French mohair rug while she read a few more chapters of *The Forsyte Saga* aloud. Then she put him in a taxi to go home and always said through the window, 'You were wonderful, darling,' as he gave her an extra fifty-dollar tip.

'You're the one I always do best with,' he would say sadly. 'I'm not very good with some of those other girls, so they do say. I'll ask for you individually next time, my dear, if I can just remember your name.'

'Lydia,' she would tell him again. It would have been exactly the same the previous week. 'Lydia. L-y-d-i-a.'

The costumes devised from the very soft brownish-beige chamois leather were barbaric and provocative. Even Mrs Jackson had had one designed for her, though almost floor-length, so she could glide around the reception rooms of the building in the evening with her sandwich tray and blend in perfectly with the décor. The walls had been newly rag-rolled an antique grey and Mr Villetto had also imported grey marble columns from Tunisia which had been put up in the vestibule, the main bath-house and the premier reception rooms. The effect was tasteful and almost royal. Against this backdrop the girls in their new costumes, and Mrs Jackson, suddenly looked like actors in a Greek melodrama.

The designer had made very short pleated skirts of natural chamois and had weighted the little hems with large black Parisian pearls hand-sewn along the lower edge. A tiny tunic, suspended from the shoulder with a baroque clasp of antique design, fluttered over the skirt and was fastened at each tiny waist with a narrow bronze belt set with more pearls slightly lighter in colour. On their feet the girls wore sandals of finely hammered terracotta-coloured leather and these fastened with narrow leather ties laced high up their very beautiful tanned legs almost to each knee. On their heads they wore golden circlets set with more pearls and they looked, suddenly, like captured princesses from a civilisation long forgotten.

'My God,' said Mr Villetto, spellbound with his hand on the till, money forgotten.

'You mean you don't like it, then.' That was the designer, anguished. The collection had taken him far longer than he had anticipated and involved sartorial principles he had never had to consider such as the wearers being entirely without underwear at all times, having to remove the garments in an instant or even being able to do their work in them in an emergency. Then there were the little cut-outs on the tunics so faintly rouged nipples could be displayed without taking away the integrity of the entire design.

'It's all absolutely wonderful.' Mr Villetto still stood with his hand on the till. 'Far far better than I ever expected. In fact, I think the whole atmosphere here has gone up several notches and I may have to arrange new charges.'

'Oh goody,' shouted Francie, one of the older women who catered for the over-sixties and provincial lawyers on holiday. 'Does this mean we don't have to bother with all those dreadful seamen on quiet nights when there isn't anyone better about?'

'Francie' — Richard Villetto could be severe when hard pressed — 'I hate to hear you call some of our very worthy customers "those dreadful seamen". You know perfectly well that Oswald only lets in the better type of ship's officer and also a few yachtsmen who actually own their own boats. You know Oswald always insists upon seeing the actual deeds to the yachts to make quite sure he's addressing the real owner and not some jumped-up waiter in a blue striped jersey.'

'I was only —' Francie began.

'Ssshhh.'

Lydia, standing at the back of the crowd, was very quiet. She and Celine usually looked after the professional customers such as lawyers and brokers, not just yachtsmen, but she still thought very wistfully of the days, a decade ago now, when she had lived far away in a large two-storeyed house with a beautiful staircase and had been considered respectable. Sometimes, on slack nights, Celine would get her to tell the story all over again of how she had been married to a nice man called Eduardo who had died and then there was the stockmarket crash, the house had had to be sold and by a series of mischances she had ended up at the Côte d'Azur.

'Tell me about the wallpaper again,' Celine would say. 'Tell me about the big room out the back where you used to arrange the flowers.' Celine had had a dramatically abused childhood in a small town down the line and had been in a dozen foster homes by the time she was fifteen when she ran away for the last time. She now possessed a hunger that was both terrible and endearing for the minor domestic details of other people's possibly calmer lives. She had been with Mr Villetto for a very long time and had been part of the very earliest beginnings of his business when he just had a fish and chip shop. Then, if high school boys came in wanting fifty cents' worth of chips, Mr Villetto would say that, for another dollar, they could look through a peephole at a naked girl. That was Celine. She used to poke out her tongue and shout various profanities that were considered nearly incomprehensible at that time and the boys would then pay another fifty cents to hear what else she might say. It was a long time ago, when four-letter words were not so usual and there was a delicious kind of novelty about spying on such a pretty, wilful, angry girl, particularly when she began to get her tattoos. She began with a large blue butterfly on her left buttock and it had just gone on from there. 'I think the punters might want more chains,' she whispered to Lydia now. 'Maybe they'll be satisfied biting the pearls off — I don't know really. My experience is that they expect black leather and chains. They do love a chain. And studs. They love really sharp studs. Are they going to pay for chamois, is what I want to know? And does it clean?'

Lydia sighed. 'How should I know?' she said. 'My only experience with chamois leather is those kind of duster things I used to wash my car.'

'You mean you had your own car? You must tell me about —'

Mr Villetto looked at them over the top of his spectacles.

'Girls,' he said, 'can we have a little quiet? There seem to be one or two people talking at the back. If we could just have everything quiet we can get on with the business of the new costumes.'

Celine put up her hand.

'Yes?' Mr Villetto looked pained.

'As a fully paid-up shop steward of the Entertainers' Collective may I respectfully suggest that we take a vote on the costumes? Otherwise I'll have to order everybody out.' These days Celine could be very militant and this tendency had been harnessed quite agreeably by Mr Villetto who had established an Armageddon Room containing replicas of war equipment. The year before last he had also purchased an outdated army ambulance with camouflage markings and four original service stretchers suspended on chains inside and this had been a real hit even though the initial problems had been almost insurmountable. The ambulance had had to be flown to the Côte d'Azur by helicopter, hired at vast expense, because the only way to get it into its present location on the second floor was to lower it from the air. The gap made in the outside wall to accomplish this was now barred with iron rods behind double-glazing and was masked by a jungle mural painted by yet another well-known artist who had wished to remain anonymous. Stockbrokers who had never seen a gun particularly adored this military room and drove away in their four-wheel drive Pajeros dazed with violence and pleasure and deeply bruised by the stretcher chains.

The clothes designer had brought three of his models with him to show off the clothes to advantage and the little draperies looked so classical and so beguiling that when the time came to vote on whether everyone wanted them it was hardly necessary.

So business settled down into a reasonably so-so run of customers, quite usual for a Wednesday night. Three or four ships' officers came in plus a yachtsman who had his left leg in plaster and said he just wanted to look. There were three stockbrokers on holiday from a city further south and a plumber from Blackpool who had come over to see his elderly mother, but had escaped from her for the evening. Two or three businessmen from smaller provincial cities arrived just before three in the morning and it was after they had all gone and Mrs Jackson was clearing up a few things around the place that she found a newspaper on one of the sofas.

No one had complained about the sudden hike in prices and none of the customers had bitten pearls off any of the costumes. The whole evening had been extremely orderly: the girls had kept their golden circlets on their heads at all times without any problems and none of the stones had become even vaguely loose. Mr Villetto began to wonder if presenting the girls as semi-royal creatures from a lost civilisation would save him the odd security fee here and there. Just sometimes a punter might become violent or abusive and he had to call a guard in but nothing like that had happened since last Easter when a visiting managing director with a chocolate allergy and necrophilia became rather peculiar after eating two Easter eggs followed by a stiff gin and tonic and then seeing Mrs Jackson silhouetted against a rising moon.

'Oh look,' said Mrs Jackson now, 'here's that paper Lydia says she used to get delivered every day. She might be interested to see it. One of those men from out of town must have left it behind.' And she went off down the corridor and through the green baize door into the private parts of the establishment. Lydia was not in her room yet so Mrs Jackson left the paper on her bed.

The elderly yachtsman was still standing out on the portico waiting for a taxi and talking about his cat. As he had not had the energy to do anything much, owing to the shocking weight of the cast, Lydia had said she would wave goodbye to him so she could think, with a clear conscience, that she had at least done him a service that evening.

There was nothing whatever in the air, no atmosphere of storm or horror, that would have prepared them for the taxing time that lay ahead. Mrs Jackson went out to the kitchen with Oswald to make a last cup of tea for the night and they finished off the lettuce and Marmite sandwiches. Mr Somerset-Smith had only picked at one or two, without his usual appetite.

'He didn't seem himself, did he?' said Mrs Jackson. 'Very peaky, I thought.'

'I went out with him to the taxi.' Oswald took a sandwich thoughtfully. 'You're quite right. He did seem peaky. I asked him if he'd had a good night and he gave that funny little creaky laugh of his and said that he'd just got Lydia to read him another chapter of *The Forsyte Saga*. Like a daughter, he said, like a daughter — just like that, kind of wheezy and breathless.'

Oswald, when he had had supper, went out to the front portico for the last time and gave it a quick sweeping with the special twig broom. He flicked a few money spiders off the hand-adzed front doors and checked for webs under the French awning. The dustcart was lumbering through the dark streets and from other less well-conducted establishments came the sound of music and screaming. The police were further down the road sorting out some kind of trouble and a couple of private security guards were bent over the gutter spitting out a few teeth. Oswald hitched up one shoulder in a superior manner, turned his back and went on sweeping. In an hour or so dawn would begin to break but meanwhile the Côte d'Azur was immaculate. Mrs Jackson had flicked a duster around intermittently all evening when punters vacated a room or the girls were busy elsewhere. The new window-cleaning company had used some kind of preparation on the glass that was guaranteed to repel all steam. The whole place glistened with elegance.

A block away the harbour lay like a dark secret and a tramp steamer slipped away from its moorings on the rising tide. There was a faint mist rising over the water and the sound of the ship's horn echoed in a melancholy way like the call of a lost creature in a forgotten sea. The injured yachtsman climbed with difficulty out of the taxi on a wharf further down the harbour basin, fumbling in his wallet for the right change and shouting goodbye as he stumped up the gangway to the deck. It seemed that everything and everybody was at last retiring or withdrawing and just for a moment the whole harbour was completely quiet.

Mrs Jackson, now in her best black silk nightdress with hand-rolled plaited straps and appliqués of guipure lace, lay back at last in her narrow but deeply comfortable little bed. It was so wonderful, in her old age, to sleep alone in a bed just big enough for one person, and to know that any stains were just droplets of tea or her own mascara which she had neglected to take off properly with removing oil. On her bedside cabinet she had placed a bottle of Moët which a punter had left in one of the cubicles. There was a good dollop of champagne left that was not too flat or stale and she poured this gently into a hollow-stemmed crystal glass made by Baccarat in the style favoured by the late Wallis, Duchess of Windsor. Mrs Jackson deeply admired the Duchess of Windsor and although she imagined she would probably die in the Côte d'Azur in this very bedsit, she hoped in her heart that a miracle could occur and she would in fact breathe her last, just like the duchess, in a tumbledown but magnificent chateau in the Bois de Boulogne with a tree growing out of the broken masonry of one chimney. With this thought occupying her mind, she drank the champagne and delicately fell asleep with the empty glass still neatly balanced on her admirable bosom.

CHAPTER
THREE

'What a ghastly night.' The following morning Claude stood at one of the upstairs windows in the house that had once been Eduardo and Lydia's home. Further along the hall the Crumlatchs were beginning to stir in what passed for the master bedroom. Kevin Crumlatch had built a walk-in wardrobe at one end of the room and, with its proportions so drastically altered, the chamber now had a truncated look not enhanced by the apricot synthetic curtains on plastic rods and a king-size bed with a duvet in electric blue to match Kevin's pyjamas.

'It was so boring.' Claude sighed heavily. 'The dog next door's at the kennels because the Smiths are away on holiday and I couldn't even go down to the shed and rattle those sheets of old corrugated iron like I used to because that moron's cleared the whole thing away. Imagine not even having a decent garden shed. Imagine having to live here without my sheets of iron to rattle. Kevin Crumlatch is a bastard. He's just a bastard.'

'Claude, I do wish you wouldn't use that language.' Florence's voice, though, contained no real reproof.

'Sorry,' said Claude.

'As I recall,' said Eduardo, 'there were always some loose tiles towards the back of the house, just above what Lydia and I used to call the morning room. Perhaps you could climb out one of the upstairs windows and rattle a few tiles out there, Claude, if you get into a rattling humour.' He sat on the fourth stair thinking deeply. 'If you did it on a rainy night you might even let some water in and make a nasty mark or two on that

35

beautiful egg-yolk yellow ceiling we all love so much.' Even Frederick fell about laughing at this.

'Oh, s-s-s-h. I know they can't hear us,' said Florence, 'but I do feel that if we make too much noise there might be some kind of vibration in the air that they'll sense somehow and I do have rather a loud laugh.'

'Rubbish.' Frederick, sitting at the head of the stairs, was seldom so terse. 'They're so insensitive they wouldn't even feel a hot iron if you branded their arms. There's nothing whatever to worry about.' He waved a laconic arm at Claude and Eduardo. 'Laugh all you like, boys,' he said. 'Feel free.'

'I know you're right, dear.' Florence went and sat beside him and held his hand.

'I'll think about the tiles, Eduardo.' Claude stared moodily out of the window. 'Thanks for the idea, but it's just not any fun here any more. There's nothing to do. Kevin Crumlatch has absolutely ruined everything. I've even tried to freeze him out of rooms just for a bit of a laugh and all he does is go and get a heater and turn it up to high.' He began to kick the skirting board.

'Don't do that, please Claude,' said Florence. 'You'll chip that wonderful glazed and hand-painted finish that was so expensive to put on. Oh sorry. I forgot he'd sanded it all off and put that shiny varnish on. Yes, Claude, do kick the skirting boards. I'm sorry, dear, I just forgot for a moment what the house is like now.'

From the bedroom came the sound of noisy yawning and stretching and Kevin Crumlatch appeared in the doorway. 'Hurry up, Moira.' His voice was even more acerbic and nasal than usual. 'It's no use sulking about the newspaper interview. You could have had a bigger part in it if you'd had something more interesting to say. I was quoted at length for the very reason that what I said was endlessly fascinating. I was not, Moira, elected national president of my retailing association for nothing. You need to get wider interests and enlarge your mind.' He padded off downstairs in his electric blue pyjamas with 'I am wonderful' printed on the back. 'I must say I'm very very surprised that no one has mentioned the interview to me. I suppose people are jealous, but I'd have expected some congratulations.' The voice was fading away now as he rounded the last bend in the stairs and went through the entrance hall to the kitchen.

After a moment or two Moira Crumlatch came out of the bedroom wearing a pair of soiled pink satin scuffs and a towelling bathrobe with a lot of pulled threads down the front. She began to cut these off in a desultory fashion with a pair of nail scissors. After stopping for a moment to look at herself in a full-length mirror with an artificial gilt frame that Kevin had bought on special somewhere she went off along the upstairs hall saying, 'Oh God, God, God.' There was another smaller mirror at the head of the staircase and she regarded herself in this for another full minute. Claude had his stopwatch out to time her. In the evening, before the moon rose, he often said things like, 'Kevin Crumlatch spent exactly nine minutes and forty-two seconds trying to comb his hair over his bald patch today.'

'Awful, awful,' said Moira as she looked at her reflection. Claude mouthed 'Sixty seconds' to Florence, who shook her head warily at him. Sometimes Claude went just too far, she thought, but he was a young man and the young were high-spirited.

From downstairs came the sound of Kevin tramping around the kitchen. 'I'm making my own breakfast, Moira,' he shouted. 'I'll be gone in twenty minutes and you can have the whole house to yourself all day to sulk in. Maybe you could try doing something to improve yourself. I noticed that they didn't use any photographs of you in the paper. This may point to the fact that you look like a dog's dinner.'

'Bastard.' Moira was walking slowly down the stairs which were now covered, wall to wall, in a slightly luminous red velvet carpeting that was entirely synthetic and contained not one shred of pure wool.

Kevin had been mystified that the house had not attracted what he called a nibble from any would-be buyer. 'I've pulled strings,' they had heard him announce to Moira, 'and I've had the odd word in the right ear and the upshot of it all is that they're sending someone to interview me about the house.'

Moira had been brushing lint from the artificial silk curtains with a plastic lint brush. 'Who?' She picked a bunch of lint off the brush and threw it out the window.

'Moira, don't do that, please.' Kevin's voice had been very cutting. 'If you continue to brush those curtains like that there'll be nothing left soon.'

'Sorry.' Moira had put the brush in a pocket of her apron. 'Who?' she had said again.

'Who what?' Kevin Crumlatch had looked at his wife over the top of his metal-framed spectacles that gave him the look of a relentless inquisitor.

'Who is coming to interview you?' Moira had given each word an equal value and they had rapped through the room.

'Goodness me,' Florence had murmured from the staircase. Moira seldom raised her voice.

Now Kevin was already halfway out of the house. 'I'll be late home tonight. I have to see a man about a dog.' He slammed the front door and stood for a few moments con-templating the day that lay ahead. He had told the office junior that he needed her at a sales conference over dinner that evening. Perhaps, he thought, she might not be entirely suspicious about the absence of anyone else till after the entrée and then, maybe, she might be very hungry and if he had ordered fillet steak for two then she just might stay and let him put his hand on her knee under the table and who knew what that could lead to. Salivating, he made his way out to the garage where Claude was hanging from a crossbeam and swinging gently back and forth, just clearing the shadow of the bonnet of Frederick's 1937 Chevrolet.

'What a pig that man is,' he told Florence when he zipped

through the wall and landed, faintly breathless, on his usual stair.

'He's planning to have it off with that poor girl who works in his office and that's why he's not going to be home till late.'

'He could be home very early then,' said Florence and continued to carefully knit the band on one of the sleeves of her favourite cardigan. 'Knit one, purl one,' she intoned, 'Knit one, purl one. Poor Moira. I do think she has a hard life.'

The newspaper interview had been a mystery to them. 'I thought, with an interview, people asked you questions and you answered,' Claude had said. Late in the day of the reporter's visit they had all sat on the stairs again to discuss it. They were quite free to inhabit any part of the house, yet the staircase remained their favourite meeting place and their most fancied place of rest. Frederick had his afternoon nap there most days but slept at night, if he did sleep, in the green bedroom at the head of the stairs. The old Sheraton revival bedroom suite that he and Florence had had in there remained mistily superimposed over the Crumlatch furniture which was of a pseudo-Scandinavian style that had been favoured back in the 1960s. The handles on its drawers were of artificial brass. The handles on the drawers and cupboard doors of Florence and Frederick's suite were made of genuine bronze in the form of Napoleonic laurel wreaths and, on her birthday, Florence made them glow eerily, just for a thrill. 'So much nicer than poor Moira's awful things,' she would always murmur as she sank back on her favourite goose feather pillow.

'I thought it was particularly disgusting,' Eduardo had added, 'when he said the garden had been completely overgrown when he came here.' There had been a long silence. 'My poor Lydia wore herself out in the garden, as we all know.'

'I did my best to help,' Claude had said.

Florence had patted his knee. 'Of course you did, dear. You made very valiant efforts. We all saw you down in the garden day after day loosening the weeds so they came out easily for her. And Frederick too — you did a wonderful job of killing all the oxalis around the boundaries with your psychic glances. We all did our best. As you all might remember I myself went around the entire house every day doing the dusting and frightening cockroaches away and also those dreadful slaters that were always inclined to come out of the panelling and die, stomach up, on the morning room carpet. We all did our best, but it was just no good. No one could have foretold the stockmarket crash and the fact that our lovely Lydia would have to sell the house and go.'

'Heaven knows where she is,' Frederick had said. 'She must be miles and miles away because, as you all know, I've searched for her endlessly with my special cosmic glasses and there's never been so much as a hint of her anywhere I've looked.' He had paused for a moment or two. 'Mind you, I have to confess to you all that my cosmic glasses are quite obsolete by now. I'm sure there must be something better on the market, something that would see much further, but my dear Florence and I — well, we've never been great ones for newfangled nonsense, have we, dear, and I'm just not sure where to get a pair. The ghosts around here' — and at this he had given a self-deprecating kind of cough — 'aren't a very modern lot, really. Nobody's very up with the play. But I can tell you with absolute authority and complete sincerity that my cosmic glasses have a range of at least two hundred miles so Lydia must be further away than that.'

Florence had begun to cry gently. 'Oh Frederick,' she had sobbed, 'as far away as that? The poor girl might as well be on the moon. And imagine him saying that our dear old house needed a substantial makeover. I've never been so hurt. And he had all our names wrong and everything.'

'Hush, hush, my dear.' Frederick had patted her arm. 'Don't upset yourself. The man simply isn't worth it.'

Now that the interview had been published and Kevin had shouted at Moira yet again, their anger was refuelled. Florence was knitting, as she always did when under stress.

'He's just a pig.' Claude glowered sourly into the middle distance. 'I'd like to harness all the energy around here and get everyone to scream at his windows and scare him to death.'

'Now Claude, dear.' Florence was wiping her eyes with a small white lace handkerchief that had been a birthday present from her best friend back in 1922. 'Two wrongs don't make a right, as I've often told you. Our real friends won't take any notice of what he said. Our real friends will know it was entirely wrong that the garden was overgrown and the house needed modernising and cleaning.'

'The trouble is' — and Frederick spoke heavily now, his expression deeply troubled — 'most of our real friends are ghosts too and none of us has any clout in the real world any more.'

'I'm absolutely sick of him,' said Claude. 'I might make the electricity fail overnight so all the bathwater's cold in the morning.' His voice had become quite eager. 'No,' he said, 'that's no good. They don't have baths in the morning. He hardly has a bath at all. He's quite a dirty man. Some days he doesn't even shave. Moira always has a bath but she just uses supermarket soap on special, and her hair shampoo's simply awful. She gets it in bulk in big plastic containers from a warehouse. You know that dog next door? Well, the Smiths use the same brand of shampoo to wash his blankets and towels, it's that bad. They wouldn't even use it to wash their dog. If I made all the water cold I'd really only be affecting Moira. But there must be something I can do to make the bastard wriggle.'

'Claude,' gasped Florence. 'Your language.'

'If only I could think of something.' Claude, for once, took no notice of his sister. 'He really made me sick the way he talked and talked all the time. Even the reporter could hardly get a word in edgeways. I think I might just waft around their bed all night and every time he goes to sleep I'll wake him up with a really freezing blast of cold air. I'll make the heater fuse if he puts it on. I've materialised once or twice just to scare him to death —'

'Claude, you haven't!' Florence dropped her knitting and it fell from stair to stair till it reached the entrance hall below.

'I have.' Claude could be quite defiant sometimes, thought Florence. 'But it's no use doing anything like that to him. He just walks straight through you. It took me a day to get over it. I felt quite peculiar.'

'Please don't do it again, Claude.' Florence was on her way down to get her handwork. 'I do hope I haven't dropped any stitches,' she murmured. 'Claude, we all know it's not good for us to have people walking straight through us. It's very diminishing for the soul — I've told you that lots of times. Every time you let someone walk through you it's like losing five years of your life. It's far worse than cholesterol or any of those other health hazards. It's even worse than smoking. Please, Claude, don't do it. You're the only brother I've got and I don't want to lose you, dear. Not again. Once was enough.'

'I know, Florence. I'm sorry. I won't do it again.' Claude was very dejected. 'It was no use anyway. As I said, he just walked straight through me. I've never had such a pain in my ribs. It was the most dreadful feeling — a cross between getting a really hard punch in the stomach and being in a lift going down quickly.'

Florence was looking very thoughtful as she picked up two dropped stitches and got her knitting under way again. 'Did that happen last Wednesday?' she said. 'I'm asking because it's just come to me that you were very quiet later last Wednesday. That was the evening you said you had a headache and went to bed early.'

'Got it in one,' said Claude. He had been picking up outdated slang again from television reruns.

'I thought it was particularly disgusting the way he boasted all the time,' said Frederick from the head of the stairs. 'Kevin Crumlatch I mean, in the interview.' He was

42

sitting on the very top stair again, just around the bend past the second landing and they could see only his feet. Frederick always wore his favourite shoes, a pair of mid-brown brogues with a very high gloss to the leather. He polished them every night before he went to bed and still stored his nugget where it was always kept, in his day, in a cupboard out beside the old back door. Everything was much altered since the Crumlatchs came to live at the house but Florence and Frederick in particular kept to the old ways. Claude and Eduardo, being younger, had adapted a little and sometimes used the Crumlatchs' modernisations. Claude said that he had seen Eduardo lying in Kevin Crumlatch's luminous blue nylon hammock which was usually strung between the two old posts that once supported a side portico that was now turned into a modern sunporch with aluminium joinery. Eduardo now said he had seen Claude sampling Kevin Crumlatch's beer from the refrigerator.

'What nonsense,' Florence said. 'Claude would never drink beer, would you, Claude? It must have been a mistake. You must just have imagined you saw Claude standing by the refrigerator drinking beer during that thunderstorm we had last week. It must have just been a trick of the light.'

Frederick cleared his throat portentously. 'I caused the thunderstorm,' he said.

'You what?' Florence dropped her knitting again.

'I caused the thunderstorm. I was so angry about Kevin Crumlatch and the way he goes on I just lost control.'

'Well, don't do it again, dear.' Florence spoke very mildly. 'It's no use upsetting yourself, I've told you that lots of times.' She sighed. 'Claude,' she said, 'are you not very comfortable, dear heart? Your expression looks quite anguished.'

'It's my back.' Claude stood up and stretched slowly. 'It doesn't ever seem to have come quite right since Kevin Crumlatch walked straight through me. I just feel all crumpled up somehow, and sometimes if I turn quickly I get this really sharp pain low down in my left shoulder.'

Eduardo spoke now. He had always been a very quiet, refined man and since he had become a ghost he had become even quieter. 'McLeod,' he said. 'Alexander McLeod's the man for you, if you've got a bad back.'

'You mean that chiropractor down on the corner in the main street?' Frederick was looking slightly alarmed. 'But if Claude's really hurt his back he won't be able to walk that far. I really will have to get the Chevy out and I find that a rather daunting thing to contemplate, what with my eyesight failing and having no licence.'

'Perhaps Mrs Thingummy could lend me her bike.' Claude often pretended he had forgotten Mrs Huddlestone's name.

'Don't be absurd, Claude.' Florence could sometimes be quite sharp. 'If you're well enough to ride a bike you can't possibly be in enough pain to bother Mr McLeod.'

'Sorry,' said Claude. 'Only kidding.'

'Why not leave it till the morning?' Frederick was always so logical and plain in all his dealings. 'We'll see how the poor boy is in the morning. You go down to the kitchen, Florence my dear, and fill up one of the old hotwater bottles for him and that might take the inflammation down. We'll have an assessment then. I do wish that you'd mentioned this sooner, Claude. It may very well have coloured my opinion about whether or not I'd make soot fall down all the chimneys again. I had decided I wouldn't because it was just too childish and unbecoming but I've changed my mind now. This is how Kevin Crumlatch gets you — you get right down to his level. If you asked me to tell you what my most salient emotion is at this very moment I'd have to truthfully state it is self-disgust.'

He went off, whistling sadly, down the stairs and through the entrance hall. After a minute or two from the old sitting room, which the Crumlatchs called the lounge, came a sound like that of small pebbles falling on a path. The hearth was marble and soot falling on it always made quite a marked noise.

'It sounds as if he's struck gold there,' said Claude as they listened to Frederick's retreating footsteps. He seemed to be heading for the old morning room out the back of the house where there was another small brick fireplace set sideways into one corner of the room.

The moon rose early that evening and sent a silvery light through the old leadlight window onto the stairwell. Frederick, having made soot fall down all the chimneys, had returned to the top stair where he sat reading the newspaper again. The page that held the Crumlatch interview seemed to float eerily in the middle of nowhere and Kevin Crumlatch, as he stepped through the front door, gave a faint cry. 'The sooner this awful creepy old house is sold the better,' he shouted to no one in particular.

Moira Crumlatch was far away upstairs in the master bedroom's en suite bathroom setting her hair on heated rollers after washing it in rosemary shampoo. She had carefully scraped the price ticket off the bottle while contemplating the shallow sham of her marriage. It occupied her mind relentlessly. She made sure every vestige of the ticket was erased because Kevin Crumlatch was not a man who liked to see evidence of large expenditure. From far away she heard his voice and, with the heated roller kit held in one hand, she made her way to the top of the stairs. 'What?' she shouted. 'Is that you, Kevin?'

'Who else would it be, bird brain.' Kevin was standing down in the entrance hall. A page from the newspaper lay innocently on the staircase. 'Moira, as true as I'm here, when I stepped in the front door that page from the paper was floating up the stairs. The draughts in this house are something else. I've spent a fortune stopping up every crack and gap and still there's enough breeze on a calm night to make a piece of newspaper float. I'm telling you, Moira, the sooner I flog this place off and make a killing the better. That is what I fleeced that widow for and that's what we're going to do.'

Eduardo waited for a moment or two before breaking down dramatically. Florence stopped knitting. Frederick rose up from his seat on the top stair and whipped swiftly down the staircase till he was beside Eduardo who had put his head in his hands and was sobbing brokenly.

'It's terrible, terrible,' murmured Florence. 'He's always taken it so very hard.'

'He'll come to terms with it one day,' said Claude, 'just like me, but it'll take time.'

'Shut up.' Eduardo's voice cracked with emotion. 'Just shut up all of you.' He stormed up the stairs and disappeared through the wall of what had once been his picture gallery and was now Moira Crumlatch's hobby room. She kept her knitting machine there and various bits and pieces of things that suggested she had taken up such activities as making quilted photograph frames out of stiff cardboard and scraps of curtain fabric, knotting macramé hangings and manufacturing notepaper out of shredded used envelopes and unpaid bills.

'Dearie, dearie me.' Frederick sighed heavily. It seemed to be an evening for people to sigh heavily, thought Florence as she sighed heavily herself. It was always very dramatic when Eduardo took on. She thought it might be partly because his mother had been an Italian war bride who had never really grown accustomed to living away from her own country. Her moods had always fluctuated and Eduardo, Florence supposed, had been brought up in an atmosphere fraught with domestic drama.

'I'll go up to him in a minute,' said Frederick. 'He won't have meant what he said. He always gets very upset if he hears Lydia mentioned like that. I'll have a word with him and he'll be all right.'

From behind the closed kitchen door came the sound of raised voices again, then breaking glass.

'I will not leave this house.' Moira Crumlatch was shouting again. Florence and Frederick stared at each other, stupefied. Moira usually let Kevin dominate her completely. 'I like living here. This is the only place I've ever lived that I've liked. I will not leave this house. If you sell it you'll have to leave me behind.'

'Don't tempt me.' In the higher octaves Kevin Crumlatch's voice became terrifyingly nasal.

'My goodness me,' said Florence mildly as she resumed knitting, 'if she really is so fond of the dear old house why did she let that awful man sand off all my lovely old eggshell paint with the swags painted by Prudence Bartholomew at the very height of her decorating career? It was quite the wonder of the town.'

Frederick, who had picked up the newspaper again and begun to read, gave a jump as Kevin suddenly shouted again. 'Don't tempt me, Moira. Leaving you behind — what a great idea.' More broken weeping from Moira echoed through the entrance hall.

'If Kevin Crumlatch decided he wanted to have all the timber scraped right back to the bone and covered with glittering varnish then who would be able to stop him, my dear?' Frederick whispered mildly to Florence as he turned a page. 'If you mentioned the words Prudence Bartholomew to him he'd probably think they were the name of a race horse.'

At this moment the kitchen door flew open and Moira Crumlatch stormed out. 'I hate you,' she shouted. 'I've hated you for years. I know perfectly well you always try to put your hand on the knee of whatever poor girl works in your office, and I know perfectly well that the latest one didn't play ball because you came home early and in a bad temper. So all I've got to say to you, Kevin Crumlatch, is ha ha ha ha endlessly on till you go deaf.' She marched out the front door and slammed it behind her.

Much later, as midnight began to strike thinly on the old town clock down in the main street, the ghosts at last all sat calmly on the stairs again, discussing the dramatic events of the evening. Eduardo, curiously cheered by the altercation in the kitchen, had come out of the old picture gallery in quite good heart. Florence and Frederick had often secretly discussed his health and had decided that perhaps one of the new wonder drugs might help his fits of depression. But, as wise old Frederick always said, the doctor they went to when they were ill had died at least a decade before wonder drugs for nerves were invented and so it was beyond his strength to prescribe them. They had all walked down to see Dr Henry at the beginning of last winter for their flu shots — these had been invented before Dr Henry died — and for some special ointment Florence needed for her hands in winter. Claude often had a check-up of a general sort due to his delicacy after having septicaemia. Frederick was usually fairly okay though he complained gently of arthritis in his hands and Dr Henry advised him to wear woollen gloves in winter if he went outside for any length of time.

'I'll knit him a pair just as soon as I've finished my pink cardigan,' Florence told him every year.

If they mentioned Eduardo's fits of depression Dr Henry just said it would be advisable to get wider interests, read the newspaper daily to enliven the mind, take a long walk every morning and try to keep his mind off things.

The evening ended in an inconclusive sort of way. Moira stayed out on the front portico till very late, sitting on the front steps with her head in her hands, crying till her face was so swollen she could hardly see. Frederick put the cosmic spectacles on and kept issuing bulletins about what was happening out there. Florence would say, 'I wonder if I should go out and see if she's all right, Frederick,' and he would reply, 'But, my dear, would she know you were there?' Kevin cooked himself toasted sandwiches but got the timer wrongly set on the machine so the house was filled with the reek of blackened cheese and burnt bread. Eduardo, more cheerful, went off to bed in what had been the upstairs library. He always slept on a very comfortable old rolled-arm couch loose-covered in Sanderson linen that used to be placed in front of the blue tiled fireplace in that room. It had now been converted into what Kevin Crumlatch called a rumpus room with an entertainment centre comprising television, stereo, video and CD player. But Eduardo still slept fairly peacefully on the old sofa whose outline was faintly superimposed over the harsh shapes of Moira's imitation leather three-piece lounge suite with matching tea trolley/coffee table.

Moira came inside quietly after she heard Kevin go upstairs.

'Oh dear,' said Florence sadly as they watched her loiter indecisively in her own entrance hall. At last she followed Kevin upstairs and there was the sound of bathwater running, then a long silence. Moira appeared in the upstairs corridor wearing a full-length nightdress made of polyester in a shade of harsh blue. It was gathered onto a high curved and collared yoke upon which was appliquéd, in polyester satin, a huge and improbable flower. The sleeves were long but ungenerous and fastened at Moira's wrists with cuffs and buttons. Wearing a pair of unattractive red felt slippers with imitation leopard-skin trimmings she went into the master bedroom, which appeared to be in darkness, and banged the door behind her.

'Oh dear,' said Florence again. 'Do you think we should put on the cosmic spectacles to —'

'Definitely not,' said Frederick firmly.

CHAPTER FOUR

D awn came slowly to the city. Mist enveloped the buildings down near the docks, including the Côte d'Azur, and from two container ships came the sound of dismal hooting as they prepared to leave port. The sea was a glassy grey but with an oily swell that hinted at a storm before evening. To the west the rain clouds were rolling in. Oswald thought he would have to get his special waterproof pale beige satin trenchcoat, only imitation Versace and made in Taiwan but almost indiscernible from the real thing, out of the back cupboard. He kept his wet weather gear near where Mrs Jackson placed her own Giorgio Armani umbrella, one rib of which was slightly bent, and a pair of Gucci loafers in grape-coloured suede.

In the meantime he flicked his special Provençal twig broom across the splendidly tiled front entrance to the Côte d'Azur and pondered, as he did most days, the events in his life that had led him to where he was now. His counsellor had told him to think of his circumstances as advantageous, which, in a real estate sense, they were. He acknowledged that.

He swept assiduously out over the pavement and went inside to get a large bucket of hot water, in which he put perfumed disinfectant, a special mixture of musk and a faint smattering of pine which Mr Villetto had obtained from a distant and mysterious spot. (He never actually said where, but the staff thought perhaps Sicily.) 'Maybe his mother sends it,' Mrs Jackson had suggested glumly as she pounded away with a heavy old-fashioned cold iron to bash the creases out of their leather costumes before a rather enervating — from the bookings anyway — Saturday night began. The wrestling championships were being held in the city and although the customers were usually quite sweet boys at heart and meant well, they did not know their own strength.

'Whatever have you been doing, Celine, to get your knickers into this state?' cried Mrs Jackson.

'Wouldn't you like to know,' said Celine sourly from her corner in the staffroom. She had picked up a book that was lying on a suede sofa — a discard from one of the upstairs entertainment rooms because it had been burnt by first-grade Cuban cigars and had some black spots on the upholstery. 'This isn't a bad story,' she said to no one in particular. 'I think this is the book Lydia reads to Mr Somerset-Smith.' The marks on the sofa had upset Oswald quite deeply at the time they were discovered. 'Probably just cigarette ash,' he had remarked grimly at the time, 'and not a Cuban cigar at all. Totally unstylish and unnecessary. Now, I could forgive Moët. I could forgive Christian Dior nail varnish. I could forgive Chanel No. 5 splashed on the sofa. But not cigarette ash, oh dear me no.' Apart from his predominantly picturesque and meaningless sweeping duties, Oswald was also in charge of upholstered furniture and there was nothing that did not attract his eagle-eyed inspection. 'Would you please try to ensure they take their shoes off?' he sometimes mildly remarked. 'I mean — this French floral chintz costs up to two hundred bucks a metre, maybe more, and I can distinctly see a footprint on this Louis Quatorze upholstered bedhead. Don't they polish the nugget off properly these days?' However, quite early in the morning on the day the storm hit the Côte d'Azur, Oswald was out the front contemplating his life. It had gone by so quickly. It seemed only a moment since he had been captain of the cricket eleven at his school and, in a moment of adolescent passion, had seriously alarmed his partner for the supper waltz at the end-of-term ball for senior students. The girl's mother, present to help serve hot sausage rolls, had calmed her daughter and then turned to Oswald.

'I'm not sure what this is about really,' she had said. 'Maybe you'd like to take me outside, behind the pavilion, and explain it all to me in very graphic detail.' She had been a large and statuesque redhead with a husband who was a neglectful bank manager fond of golf. That had been, perhaps, the beginning of it all, he thought rather wistfully now. She had confided in her best friend who had confided in her best friend who had passed the news on to her best friend and so it had gone on till now. Oswald had never gone to university, as he had planned, to become a marine biologist though, as for that, there was a lot of water in the Côte d'Azur. The marble-edged swimming pool with genuine eighteen-carat gold-plated taps accurately shaped like dolphins held hundreds of gallons of specially filtered water and he was personally in charge of strewing the pink rose petals on it when there was a booking for the bath-house. He also tested the chlorine levels three times daily and sprayed all the pool draperies with aerosol glitter twice each evening. Cheered by these marine thoughts he wandered off down the street to investigate exactly what had happened last night at the Pinkney Pelle Parlour where he thought he had seen a fight in the small hours.

Peregrine, the doorman there, was obviously still asleep somewhere on the premises because his pale orchid-coloured Honda City was parked crookedly over the kerb, its artificial ponyskin upholstery looking decidedly tacky in the early morning mist. Oswald rang the doorbell to no avail so flicked around the approach to the parlour with his broom for a moment or two. It didn't hurt, he thought, to be a bit kind to the neighbours from time to time, though it might be rather over the top to take down the cobwebs above the front door's architrave. He stood for a time staring deeply into the gutter at several small squarish white objects which he thought might be teeth. Poor old Hector the security guard, he thought, would be minus a few more molars so it would be back to Mr Amras Singh, the immensely discreet dentist who had chambers just off the main street and was famous, in an in-house kind of way, for patching them all up. Even Mr Villetto had a false front tooth, absolutely undetectable from the real thing, made years ago by Mr Amras Singh in the days when Mr Villetto's establishment was somewhat rougher and clients sometimes threw things. A can of beer, not even chilled, had collected Mr Villetto neatly on the upper front jaw. These days he served only Moët and possibly the better chardonnays or semillion sauvignon blancs when airline pilots and successful commercial travellers were in town. Parliamentarians in general had very poor taste in wine so he kept an emergency supply of a relabelled müller thurgau for them. But the tooth incident had taught him never to serve the wine himself. Usually Mrs Jackson attended to the serving of any drinks now and a basilisk glance from her deterred any tendency by clients to become effervescent.

'Disgusting,' murmured Oswald and prodded at one of the white things with the handle of his broom. Yes, it certainly was a tooth. He ran his tongue experimentally around his own teeth, happily all there and in lovely order even after all these years. He thought again of his counsellor who had said, with an air of penetrating earnestness, that he was a fortunate man to live so easily and to have free accommodation so well placed for everything the metropolis could offer. 'Oswald,' she had said, 'you are a lucky man. Believe me when I say this — there are thousands of heavily mortgaged people paying heftily for pied-à-terres no bigger than your bedsit, possibly even smaller. I have actually driven past your emporium and it isn't half bad, Oswald, architecturally speaking. Almost the Spanish Mission style, I would have said. And you have a sea view? Yes?' She had made a few arithmetical calculations on a small piece of paper ripped from her personal handbag diary. 'Oswald, that adds another ten thousand dollars to the price of your free eyrie if you had to pay for it. My advice is to just be happy. Take advantage of what your life offers and cease to worry about what it may have been. Think of it this way — on your first excursion into the deep as a marine biologist you could have drowned.'

'I see,' Oswald had said doubtfully but with a dawning sense of happiness and ease. He paused for a long time while the counsellor waited. Oswald had such a beautiful profile, she thought, particularly when he was wrestling with inner problems. 'What's an emporium?' he had asked at last.

'A shop,' she had said.

'I see.' Oswald's expression had brightened. 'A knocking shop — oh yes, I do see now. Thank you very much, Miss Simmonds,' he said and shook her hand gratefully before leaving. Further down the street, on his way back to the Côte d'Azur, he had looked at the piece of paper she had given him with her calculations and seen that it also contained her private telephone number.

He stood now regarding the teeth in the gutter and also thinking about Miss Simmonds. She was quite a good-looking broad, he thought, though not exactly very young. From the faint wrinkling of her wrists and the lack of tactile elasticity in the skin of her hands he would put her at about fifty-two. Fifty-two, though, was a good and mellow age, he thought, salivating gently. He would not mind being fifty-two again himself. Hector, the doorman at the Pinkney Pelle Parlour, was sixty-two. Oswald himself was approaching an age he did not like to contemplate. But at least he still had all his teeth, he thought with a sense of faint satisfaction, and then, in a moment of extreme friendliness towards the battered and possibly unconscious Hector, raised the Provençal broom and officially swept away all the cobwebs and dirt that adorned any part of the parlour's facade he was able to reach.

'There you are, my friend,' he said and marched up the street to the Côte d'Azur, stopping for a minute or two to regard the building with satisfaction. With his broom held quite tenderly in hands that were shaking with hidden emotion, Oswald stepped into the darkly beautiful entrance hall that was almost completely upholstered in rare silk and at that exact moment a terrible scream rent the air. The chandelier tinkled and one prism shattered. Dropping his broom, Oswald ran madly up the staircase, his desperately thudding feet irrevocably marking the slate blue velvet carpet. It sounded like Lydia's voice, he thought, and headed for the east wing where she had a small apartment exquisitely furnished with French antiques, most of them miniature apprentice pieces because the area was so tiny. Her bedside cabinet was only as high as the smallest poodle but, as she kept all her money in the bank, this was of no consequence. She kept only odd change in its tiny drawers, plus a small diamond watch in the Cartier style with a black velvet strap.

The sounds of distress had ceased. An eerie silence descended on the building, broken only by the sound of doors opened by various girls, most of them yawning and hastily arranging robes of various sorts around their voluptuously naked bodies. Celine's robe, of dusky pink damask, had been brought from Paris earlier in the year by a devoted client. Its lapels were patterned with mythical birds whose golden plumage had been embroidered in satin stitch by pre-pubescent girls. Two trainees called Phyllis and Jane, who had tumbled out of the already wide open door of their shared bedsitter, were just carelessly bundled up in tartan towelling bathrobes, floor-length and with matching fringed ties. Phyllis had a small emerald nose stud and both Jane's eyebrows were pierced with six sterling silver rings in various sizes, each one set with a small ruby. They seldom removed these except by particular request from one customer who required completely unadorned bodies — and two at once.

Mrs Jackson had awakened in such a fright that she sat up immediately without fully comprehending her situation. She had slept very peacefully through the remnants of the night with the empty champagne glass balanced on her commodious bosom but it now flew through the air and smashed on the marble floor. Had she been lying six inches further down in the bed the glass would have landed on a deeply

55

luxurious Chinese rug that lay beside her narrow little antique bed. Its wooden sides enclosed her kindly and the lavender-scented bedlinen itself, gleaming white and faintly starched, held a peculiar and delicious innocence which, in her retirement, she felt she deserved. She slept sweetly and daintily now, like an old baby.

'Are you all right, Geraldine?' Oswald opened the door of her small apartment without even knocking. They had known each other for more than half a lifetime and in such strange situations that Oswald did not even stop to think of formalities. He was the only person in the city's entire entertainment industry who ever called Mrs Jackson Geraldine. Her clients had called her only darling and then solely at the height of passion.

Geraldine Jackson had rescued Oswald once from the clutches of the immensely rich and frighteningly possessive Mrs Lillian Anstruther who, more than thirty years ago, had become so enamoured of him that she actually nailed him into her Bentley, then nailed the garage doors shut and nailed herself into her marital-settlement mansion on the Golden Mile. Mrs Jackson had attended to that small matter with mysterious fortitude and equally mysterious success and by four o'clock on the day after the incident Oswald was back home again in the premises then occupied by the Côte d'Azur. He had a small cut, already healing, on his left temple, rope burns on his wrists, a few tiny holes here and there but already scabbing nicely and painful soles owing to the fact that Mrs Anstruther had also glued his feet to the floor of the car and every layer of skin had been torn from them in his escape. But basically he was fine.

Mrs Jackson had buckled on her French black trenchcoat, pulled a beret over her left eye at a rakish and very becoming angle and walked jauntily off down the street, saying she would see about Oswald and would be back within the hour, which she was. She had been slightly out of breath, had lost or mislaid the beret and Mr Villetto had noted that her silk shirt, on the right way when she went out, was now inside out. Judge Anstruther, hearing a flamboyant murder case at the time, was rumoured to have called for an adjournment shortly after Geraldine Jackson left the Côte d'Azur but the facts were very blurred and everyone had been so glad to see Oswald and curious to see the nail holes that they had forgotten about the other details. Mrs Jackson had simply said, 'I'll go and put the kettle on.'

Oswald, in his turn, had rescued Mrs Jackson by exotic means from a serial killer who had strangled three charmingly accommodating girls just off a busy road at the top of town about twenty years ago. As a result she had a small blurred scar on the left side of her throat plus an abiding horror of high brick walls and men in pinstriped suits. This was back when Richard Villetto had much smaller premises and the staff were allowed to attend to their nocturnal business, mostly standing up, in the parking lots, doorways and little parks nearby.

Oswald, emotionally incapable of working ordinarily for several months after the Anstruther incident, used to do the rounds each evening to collect money and maybe take a few cheese and lettuce sandwiches to girls who were nearly dead on their own, or strange men's, feet. On just such an evening he noticed that Geraldine Jackson was missing among the tombstones of a nearby cemetery for longer than was necessary and went to find her. His palpitatingly sincere evidence and the indelible mark left by one of his sandwiches pressed deeply into the fibre of the alleged murderer's suit were each sufficiently telling to result in a conviction. Mrs Jackson always said to Oswald that it would have been nice if Selwyn Anstruther had been able to hear the case because she would not have minded his knowing the intimate details, particularly the bit about the tattoos up her inner thighs, but sadly he had sudden and pressing business in the Bahamas for more than two months. He sent her unsigned postcards but she recognised his block capitals immediately, and he brought her back a beautiful gift of black pearl earrings in the largest size available. Lillian, his ex-wife, had by then been put into special care.

Most of these historical facts were known by the staff but were far from their minds as the sound of breaking glass in Mrs Jackson's room arrested the flight of everyone running up the stairs on the morning of Lydia's hysteria. They crowded into the doorway as Oswald strode forward to rescue Geraldine Jackson from her tumbled bed which was islanded by broken glass.

'Have you got a good stout pair of leather-soled slippers?' asked Oswald, regarding the myriad fragments of smashed crystal.

'Of course not, you moron,' Mrs Jackson replied in a mock-angry tone. She and Oswald had known each other for so long they often spoke in this seemingly savage manner to each other. 'What would I be doing with a pair of good stout leather-soled slippers I ask you? Me in my profession?' Even at her advanced age Mrs Jackson could still toss her head with voluptuous recklessness. Oswald took a step back. My God, he thought, she's still a very handsome woman.

'All I've got,' said Mrs Jackson, 'as you very well know, Ossie, are my feather-trimmed French velvet high-heeled mules in various pastel shades including butter yellow. Then, of course, there are my evening shoes mostly in black satin, one pair with heels hand-painted with gold spider webs, and various pairs of sandals that tie in bows at the ankle. But no stout leather-soled slippers, Ossie, no. I actually think I've got only one pair of shoes to wear during the day and they're those suede loafers miles away downstairs —'

'Can we get on with this?' shouted Celine aggressively.

'— but as I'm mostly only up and about at night in the reception rooms I never feel I need any more,' went on Mrs Jackson, undeterred. 'The only place I go in the daytime is over to that shop I like, that one where I have afternoon tea on my day off, Ossie, and my purple suede Gucci loafers do for that.'

'Has anyone got a plank?' This suggestion came from a sensible but very pretty girl who was originally from a dairy farm where she had actually milked cows.

'What a good idea.' Oswald stared around. Planks did not abound at the Côte d'Azur but he gave a shout of triumph and dragged a finely woven Hamadan carpet runner into the bedroom. Within a moment of the rug being thrown down Mrs Jackson had joined the rest of the gang and they continued rushing up the stairs.

'Do wait,' panted Mrs Jackson. 'I really need to get these mules on properly. I got a size 6B when I really need a 7. Usually I can get away with them being a bit tight but at moments like this —'

'Belt up,' shouted Celine as she sprinted ahead. 'Why don't you just button up?' Her mother had worked as a tailoress and sewing terminology came easily to her.

'Well, really.' Mrs Jackson's surprise was assumed only for effect. She knew, in her heart, that Celine's disturbed upbringing caused her to speak roughly when she was deeply moved by emotion, so she was not offended.

But there were more cries coming now from further down the corridor and the others broke into a run, leaving Mrs Jackson to teeter along on her four-inch heels.

'It's definitely from Lydia's room,' she called. 'Whatever can the matter be? It's not poor Mr Somerset-Smith having a turn because I saw him leave with my very own eyes and Lydia told me he'd been very calm. All she did was read to him and then he went off home. Oswald saw him, didn't you, Ossie?' They all had a secret fear, seldom uttered but understood throughout the establishment, that Mr Somerset-Smith would die one evening while visiting the Côte d'Azur, probably with his knees locked, and the difficulty of explaining his posture to coroners, doctors and perhaps visiting police exercised all their minds.

'I think what I'd do,' Celine used to say while she blew lazy smoke rings through her finely chiselled nostrils, 'if the old boy croaked while he was, you know, with me, so to speak, I'd jump straight out the window and hide in the park all night till I saw the whole thing was over — you know, police, doctor, ambulance, hearse, the lot. Then I'd come back.'

'For heaven's sake,' Mrs Jackson had snapped at her, 'definitely not the park, Celine. Just go along to the Pinkney Pelle and spend the evening there, dear. Do a bit of moonlighting or, if it's a Wednesday, you could quietly get a martini on credit in the bar and listen to Delwyn Le Fanu, that resident jazz singer they've got. Her high notes aren't very reliable but she packs a real punch in the lower registers. I don't think anyone could be bettered, for instance, singing middle C. And her frocks are always worth a look.' She fell into a slight reverie. 'I do wish she'd give me the name of her dressmaker. I've never known anyone make a dress out of just one hanky before. But please promise me you won't hide in the park, dear.'

But now the crowd had reached Lydia's door and they clustered outside as if suddenly shy. From inside the room came the sound of dramatically broken-hearted sobbing and a rustling noise like that of a newspaper when its pages are turned.

'I might be too old,' Mrs Jackson said as she reached them.

'Too old?' Oswald looked bewildered. 'Whatever do you mean, Geraldine?' He used her Christian name only in moments of extreme formality or informality.

'Too old to have that dressmaker make me a frock out of just one hanky.'

'All you ever do is think about yourself. Self first, self second, self third and if there's anything left over it's self again.' Celine seemed more enraged than ever. 'There's a terrible emergency here with Lydia and you're talking about dresses made out of hankies. Let's get our priorities right here and maximise the opportunity to work together for the common good.'

'Sorry.' Mrs Jackson hung her head to hide the tears of shame in her faded but still lovely eyes.

At this stage a stentorian voice bellowed through the building. It came from Mr Villetto on one of his morning inspections of the premises.

'Can anyone tell me where everybody is?' His voice cracked slightly as it took on a higher note for the next question. 'And could someone be kind enough to also tell me why one of my best champagne glasses is lying smashed on the floor of Geraldine Jackson's bedroom even though I have expressly forbidden their being moved from my Chippendale cocktail cabinet? And is anyone aware of the fact that the aforementioned glasses were sent to me by my Aunt Marcella who married the head of the Paris Mafia in 1947? And who actually pays the bills round here? Hmmm?'

CHAPTER
FIVE

The following morning, as they all journeyed southward in a hired double-decker bus, Mr Villetto was in a more genial mood, sitting in the front seat behind the driver and roughing out the first draft of a letter to the Baccarat factory. He set it out as a kind of order form and from time to time consulted Mrs Jackson about whether it would be advisable to order three extra glasses in each category of size and function or to go for a half dozen. The younger girls had been singing merrily in unison since the bus left the motorway. Celine had brought a ghettoblaster but they had not turned it on yet because they had been so happy singing some simple country songs that were mostly about innocent women who were standing up. 'Waltzing Matilda' was a favourite — they had sung this three times, right through all the verses and with the chorus fully done each time.

'That's about enough, I think,' said Mr Villetto quickly as they were about to begin all over again and, tapping the bus driver on the shoulder, he gestured towards a grocery shop on a corner just past an overgrown hedge. 'I think we'll stop up ahead,' he said, 'and I'll get the girls an ice cream or something, anything to shut them up.'

'Not a chocolate cornet,' said Noeline. 'That stockbroker I see on a Monday's got this thing about chocolate cornets. What he likes to do is tear all the suspenders off my black leather sequin-encrusted corselette and —'

'Please, Noeline.' Mrs Jackson used an admonishing tone very like Mr Villetto's over the business of the smashed glass. 'Have you no dignity whatever?' She nodded her head in a secretive manner towards three girls from the Pinkney Pelle who had decided to come on the expedition as union delegates and observers. 'We don't want them to learn all our trade secrets, now do we.'

At the shop Mr Villetto decided to purchase ice cream slices for the girls because their slim square shape and pink wafers brought on no fits of erotic recollection. As far as he knew, no ice cream slice had ever been used in the entertainment industry for anything other than a little snack at interval at the cinema. Chocolate trumpets were a different matter entirely, particularly with walnut topping and, with union delegates on board the bus, he was anxious not to provoke a crisis of any kind.

He sat down on a large log of wood that had been placed outside the shop as a countrified bench and leaned back in the sunshine of a truly lovely summer's day. Had it not been for the tiny but elegant figure of Lydia, the star of his establishment, still crumpled dejectedly in her seat on the bus, he would have felt divinely happy. His wife had decided to stay at home because she had eighty ladies coming for a fully catered lunch that was to include roast swan, with truffle pâté as an entrée. After that the ladies would play bridge for the afternoon, fighting like hellcats over who had gone no trumps. He sighed with satisfaction at the idea of missing such domestic trauma. By the time he arrived home again his wife would have had her cloth-of-gold apron dry-cleaned and any little diamonds that had fallen out of the halter neck would have been speedily re-set by his own private jeweller.

He sat contentedly in the summer sunshine mulling over the multifarious facts of his life that had led him to his present happy situation of being in charge of so many lovely girls. The faint hint of approaching autumn did nothing to dim his appreciation of his own remarkable career. Celine had found a large ball somewhere on the steps leading up to the shop's small verandah and he watched the girls tossing the ball from one to another, their beautiful nubile limbs glowing like ivory against the backdrop of the emerald grass. Everything was verdant and beautiful, the massive heads of blue hydrangeas nodding over the fence nearby like the faces of proud old mothers. Celine had had her long, delicately boned legs heavily tattooed with various emblems and mottoes, some of them unprintable so that the tattooist had used a flowing Gothic script to inscribe the immortal words of delicious piquancy, and as she and the other girls pranced about two large trucks drew to a sudden halt. Mr Villetto went over and had a word with both the drivers. 'The girls are having a day off,' he called up into one of the cabs, 'but anytime you're in the city you and your colleague can book in for a night of pleasure if you're owner-drivers.' He handed up one of his cards and waved both the trucks on. 'The entry fee is a hundred bucks and that just gets you in the door,' he called after them. 'And you'd need to have a lounge suit with current lapels and designer-label formal shirt and tie, preferably pure silk. No jeans or T-shirts allowed except for Calvin Klein originals and preferably Gucci loafers or something simi —' He was interrupted by one of the trucks backfiring. 'What impertinence,' he shouted and went and sat down again on the log. Things seemed quieter after the trucks drove away, one of them wavering and almost hitting a power pole. That driver, Mr Villetto thought, had been most deeply affected by Celine's specialised loveliness, going a funny colour and murmuring in an unintelligible manner while trying to cope with a marked facial tic. He sat deeply appreciating the beauty about him — the girls, the flowers, the loveliness of the countryside — and pondered the events of the previous day that had resulted in this strangely unexpected journey into the countryside.

Yesterday Mrs Jackson had slipped and ricked her left ankle as they had approached Lydia's room. From within they all heard the sound of tragic sobs. Several of the girls went back along the corridor to pick Mrs Jackson up, and Samsonette, a muscular girl who specialised in rocking very small men dressed in baby clothes to sleep on Nursery Night, tossed her nonchalantly over one shoulder for the last few yards.

'Don't forget to pick up my Dolce et Gabanna blue feather-trimmed mules with rhinestone buckles,' murmured Mrs Jackson anxiously. 'They only cost a hundred and fifty dollars on special because I take such a small size but —'

'We'll get them later,' shouted Celine. 'How can you think about such frivolity at a time like this.'

Mr Villetto turned the antique Sèvres door handle, its ormolu mountings shining delicately in the light from a small Waterford chandelier that was kept on night and day to illuminate the shadowy velvet luxuries of the third floor. The chartreuse silk curtains and festoon shades in Lydia's delicately luxurious bedroom were still tightly drawn over the windows but they could make out a crumpled figure on the Louis Quatorze bed. Hunched against the damask-upholstered headboard and oblivious to the delicacy of the carvings and inlays, Lydia reclined with what looked like a page from a newspaper crushed to her left breast.

She was wearing a full-length nightdress designed on Grecian lines with a transparently draped bodice trimmed with blue silk velvet forget-me-nots. On the second toe of one of her pale slim feet she wore a large but delicately set diamond solitaire ring and her toenails were immaculately painted in a shade of deepest mushroom pink with a pearl finish.

'Whatever is the matter, Lydia, my dear child?' Mrs Jackson said from her perch against Samsonette's shoulder. Her voice was somewhat muffled because her face was pressed into Samsonette's imitation leopard-skin drapery with genuine suede piping, made by a former tailor who had taken to professional pugilism late in life and was now in a home for retired wrestlers and boxers. Wordlessly Lydia handed her the page from the paper and Mrs Jackson began to read aloud. A terrible silence fell on them all as they realised the awful significance of what they were hearing.

'"Kevin and Moira Crumlatch knew they were in trouble the moment they walked on to the deeply overgrown grounds of 10 Fleming Street,"' read Mrs Jackson in a voice that faded away in accents of sudden horror and surprise. 'But, Lydia,' she said, eyeing the sobbing figure on the bed, 'wasn't that your old house, dear, the one you've always told us about?'

The sobbing increased in intensity.

'You said the garden was beautiful, you liar.' Celine, always inclined to become swiftly aggressive, stepped forward and snatched the newspaper.

'It was, it was.' Lydia's voice was very faint and blurred by tears. 'The garden was beautiful, just like I said. Read the rest. It's awful.' She drew the French lace-trimmed sheet over her face and lay like a statue beneath its folds. 'It's all fibs.' She began to cry again. 'I left it in beautiful order.'

Mrs Jackson gave a slight scream because the recumbent form reminded her suddenly and horribly of the stone effigies in the cemetery the evening of her own near-death experience with the would-be murderer.

To Mr Villetto, sitting in the sun while the girls ate their ice creams, it seemed hardly a moment since the reading of the appalling story, the vote by all the girls to go on strike till further notice, a further vote to personally picket Lydia's old house as a protest against false allegations of untidiness and dirtiness and the journey southward by hired luxury double-decker bus after a night of fitful sleep. Yet, as he sat there quietly crunching his own pink biscuit wafers, he could see that within the framework of the disastrous story about Lydia's old residence there were marvellous benefits. They would all have a short break away from the rigours of their usual lives, the customers would have to wait for the usual comforts so might pay more for them, the decorators could be called in to do a quick paint job on the downstairs cloakrooms and the carpet shampoo man could have at least three clearly unpopulated days to clean all the carpets and get them properly dry. He had also decided to call in the firm that came twice a year to sharpen the nails in the torture cupboards so they left only pinpricks, not bruises, on the bodies of anyone who wanted to be locked in. The whole area could be recalibrated too, he thought, so that the computerised mechanism that assessed the size of each customer was completely accurate. It would not do, he thought as he picked up his cellphone to make the call, to puncture anyone really seriously.

'Just a word, Don,' he said when his call was answered in a discreet whisper by a man with a lisp. 'Rick here. The girls and I have come away for a day or so. Just thought you might like to nip in — you've got your own key, haven't you? — and check on the Armageddon Room, please. I think all the whips are fine but just check the handles, will you, and the thongs? Some of them might be a bit worn and possibly, shall we say, soiled? Celine does get rather carried away from time to time and even though the punters like to be lashed till the blood runs — well, need I say more than that, Don? No, indeed. Just have a peek and see if anything needs releathering and maybe have a look at the torture cupboards. Perhaps some of the nails might need resharpening. And cast your eye over the chains if you would, please. I don't think we've got any rust but you never know. Some of those brokers are surprisingly well-built for fat-cat wimps in cushy jobs so you'll need to check the breaking strain with the calibrator. Don't know they're alive, do they, Don — ha ha ha. Thanks a lot. See ya.'

By a ghastly coincidence someone from Lydia's old town must have visited the city and left the newspaper behind at the Côte d'Azur. By mischance she had read the story and had fallen into a state of deep depression.

Mr Villetto went over to the bus and tapped on the window to attract her attention. 'Are you sure you won't have an ice cream?' he called through the sunproof glass. 'I don't think you've had a thing to eat since you saw that awful story.'

Lydia looked at him sadly and shook her head. 'No, thank you, Mr Villetto,' she said in her clear little bell-like voice, and turned her face away.

He returned to his perch on the large log. It was no wonder the punters paid so much for her, he thought happily. She had such class, such delicacy, such sensitivity. And her much-discussed reputation for extreme ruthlessness under pressure ensured that there was never any trouble in her part of the house. Mr Somerset-Smith, the oldest and most notable client at the Côte d'Azur, always said she was like his daughter if only he had had one and that was a compliment indeed, Mr Villetto thought, because a Miss Somerset-Smith would have been one of the most gently reared and beautifully presented women it would have been possible to meet. He gazed contentedly about the pastoral scene while the bus driver read *Best Bets*, Lydia repaired her make-up and the girls ran about gathering wild flowers to put in their hair. Mrs Jackson was tying up Samsonette's great mane of reddish-blonde curls with a long piece of French silk ribbon in a leopard print and twining brilliant yellow dandelion blooms among the bows and tendrils. Her busy fingers, hardly worn at all by the passage of the years, were immaculately manicured for the journey. Paling a little, Mr Villetto now recalled the latest account for all the girls' weekly manicures plus a new bottle of nail varnish each in a colour of their own choice. Mrs Jackson had selected a shade of pale plum crossed with wild rose. Some of the younger girls, who included two brilliant and beautiful part-time workers studying law and atomic science at university — their textbooks were just so expensive, they said, rolling their eyes during their interview — had chosen black or luminous green with a tinsel finish.

As the girls played innocently beside the luxury bus Mr Villetto could still hear, echoing mystically in his mind, the sound of Lydia's sobs as Mrs Jackson finally read aloud every word of the newspaper story that said Lydia's old house had been unkempt when she sold it.

'It wasn't, it wasn't.' That was all Lydia would say till at last the doctor was called to give her a tranquillising injection. Mrs Jackson sat by her bedside, ashen-faced, then crept away to pack a small Louis Vuitton valise with a few necessities such as a silk negligée with a fluffy lining in case the nights were chillier further south, a diamond bracelet with mostly genuine stones though the colour was somewhat yellow and some cosmetics.

Never before had the entire staff of the Côte d'Azur gone on holiday together and on no other occasion had he ever placed a billboard saying 'Closed Until Further Notice' on the main door. Even Oswald, having swiftly packed a tartan grip bag, had come along on the excursion and he now appeared at the back of the bus, removing dust and a few dead leaves from the back windows with his Provençal broom. As Mr Villetto watched, Oswald opened the door of the luggage compartment to check on the signs that had been made swiftly but expertly by the signwriter who worked for the Côte d'Azur's clothes designer. From where he sat beside the road Mr Villetto could quite easily read their messages.

WHAT A WHOPPER
DO NOT EVER SAY ANY OF US HAS A DIRTY HOUSE
DISORDERLY — YES. DIRTY — NO
ENTERTAINERS' UNION PROTEST AGAINST DEFAMATION

And so on. The signwriter had recycled parts of old notices at the fashion house, mainly pertaining to sales or reductions on the more avant-garde type of evening wear from the house's Sharon Stone phase the year before last. All the old lettering had been disguised with French terracotta-coloured paint and some of the notices still had their original gilded frames, which gave the projected protest a somewhat luscious and luxurious look.

Samsonette had begun to drill some of the younger girls in certain dance routines she planned to execute outside Lydia's old house the following day to stop the traffic in Fleming Street, or at least slow it to a crawl. But several cows came to a near-by fence and any cars passing the old shop seemed to swerve alarmingly even though the highway was reasonably straight for several hundred metres, so Mr Villetto at last gave the signal to depart. Possibly, he thought, reluctantly, it was time to give up this sylvan idyll and take to the open road again. They were only a little over halfway to Lydia's old town and there were many kilometres to travel before darkness came down upon them.

Celine, as chief union delegate, blew her whistle and shouted, 'Everybody in,' so, in a colourful and laughter-filled gaggle, the girls all climbed on board the bus again, falling silent only when they saw Lydia still crumpled in her seat. During their joyful sudden freedom in the countryside they had, just for a moment, forgotten her anguish. Their departure was delayed for only a few minutes while Mr Villetto rang his wife on the cellphone. 'Pretty baby,' they heard him say. 'How —'

There seemed to be a lot of indeterminate shouting coming from the other end of the line.

'Sank?' said Mr Villetto at last. 'But, darling one, wasn't it stuffed? Oh dear — not stuffed enough. Just stuffed with a lemon? This seems extraordinary.' He put his hand over the receiver and addressed the girls. 'Ambrosia says the swan fell in on itself because it wasn't stuffed firmly enough and two of the guests missed out on meat entirely.'

More scratchy noises came from the telephone. 'What was that, my darling?' said Mr Villetto in a somewhat frightened voice. Ambrosia's fits of rage were legendary, unsuitable for real life but admirably fitting for a Wagnerian heroine if only Ambrosia had had the voice to be one on stage. 'What did you say, my sweetness and light?' He seemed to listen for a long time. 'I see, darling one. A whole Parma ham delivered by special courier? And why not, indeed. My little sweetheart' — Ambrosia weighed in at just under sixteen stone — 'must have a nice lunch with her friends. A tiny little ham is neither here nor there. Please, my teensy-weensy sweetheart, don't think for another moment about the catering costs.' Looking slightly pale, he terminated the call and as the bus drew away from the old country store he spoke in a low voice to Mrs Jackson. 'How long do you think we'll be away on this jaunt?'

'At least three days.' Mrs Jackson had a silk handkerchief crushed into her right hand and was polishing a secondary pair of pearl earrings she had brought with her as a back-up in case her best ones looked too ostentatious. 'Maybe four,' she said, 'depending on how things go.'

'Excellent.' Mr Villetto settled into his seat a little more comfortably. Whatever had happened in his Tuscan-style residence today would mercifully not be fully revealed to him for possibly a hundred hours or more. In that time Ambrosia would have cooled down, the caterers would have taken all the dishes away and there would have been at least one more bridge party somewhere else to take Ambrosia's mind off the collapsing swan. He had forgotten to ask her about the truffle entrée but that might be a suitably safe topic of conversation for tomorrow when he clocked in for his daily report about the family.

In the meantime the bus travelled resolutely southward, drawing nearer and nearer to Lydia's old house, which still lay secretly within the enfolding branches of massive trees. It had only ever been possible to see the tallest of the chimneys at the front of the house above the burgeoning branches of magnolias and maples. Sometimes, perhaps in autumn when the leaves began to fall from the copper beech trees, you could see the glimmer of a leadlight window here and there on the front of the house and in the depths of winter, when all the trees, gaunt and leafless, stood in skeletal ranks beside the old driveway, you might catch a glimpse of the front portico. In the early hours of many mornings, after the girls had farewelled the last of the clients and had dabbed iodine on various small puncture marks on their torsos if they had been working in the torture room, they had all listened spellbound to Lydia's simple tales of her former home. It glittered in their minds like a brilliant mirage, infinitely precious. To think they were now actually travelling towards it at last caused a reverent silence to slowly fall upon them all.

CHAPTER
SIX

Back at the big house on the promontory things were not happy. The tiles on the back wing had been rattling for hours even though there was no wind, and Moira and Kevin Crumlatch had had another domestic incident.

'Oh Kev, Kev,' she had sobbed brokenly sometime during the previous night, 'this is the only place I've ever been happy, where I've really come into myself and become enlarged as a personality. Kevin? Are you listening? It's only in this exact house I've felt my spirit rise up from the broken thing it had become. I've become attuned to my inner self here, Kevin. Please don't sell this house and make me go somewhere else. Please —' But she had got no further than that.

'Moira,' said Kevin in a very tired voice, 'you've been reading those personal motivation books again and I've already told you they make me want to vomit. By all means talk like that to your batty friends but don't bore me with it.'

He went into the spare bedroom, the one where two floor-boards were loose and where the ghosts kept a few precious remnants of their old lives, slammed the door vigorously and seemed to be settling down for the night on the spare bed. Silence settled on the house again, apart from a few more broken sobs from Moira who was curled up under the luminous duvet.

Frederick put on the spectral spectacles so he could look through the wall at her. 'She's crying again,' he intoned. 'Her mascara's run all over the pillowcase. Now she's wiping her eyes on a lime green tissue. Now she's stopped crying. Now she's curling up again in a foetal position and going to sleep.'

'Thank you, Frederick,' said Florence wearily. 'I think we've got the picture.' From far away down the valley came the sound of the town clock striking two in the morning. 'The thing I find most upsetting, in a small kind of way,' she continued as she began the neckband of the pink cardigan, 'is that one just doesn't sleep properly any more.' She was sitting up now in the rosewood bed with boxwood inlays that had always been in the front bedroom upstairs. It was now super-imposed over the unattractive pseudo-Scandinavian bedroom suite that Moira and Kevin had placed in the room when they moved in. The tops of the matching bedside cabinets had a plastic finish so nothing could mark them but, from time to time, Claude, calling upon terrestrial sonic strength which he had studied for decades and was only now able to harness effectively, had burnt marks on the edges with his fingers. The Crumlatchs would often have a row about which of them had started smoking again and had sneaked into the spare room to have a fag without the other knowing. Claude, dangling from the lantern in the stairwell, would laugh horribly at the sound of their discord.

'Sometimes I do think Claude is just a tiny bit naughty,' Florence remarked lovingly and mildly on one of these occa-sions as Kevin Crumlatch, wearing a mystified expression as well as a burnt orange polyester shirt with Konstant-Kreese trousers and grey shoes that fastened with Velcro, came out on to the top landing to say, 'Moira, I think we've got crows or magpies in the garden. I think I can hear them screeching.'

Claude, however, had also spent a restless night owing to his internal injuries and he was now pacing the upper hall-way. 'We really will have to do something, Frederick,' said Florence, putting her knitting down. 'I do think we'll have to take him down to the chiropractor and what better time than now when there's not much traffic about and no one will see us. Claude?' she called. 'Come in here for a minute, please dear.'

74

Claude appeared in the bedroom doorway, his left arm held against his chest. He had a pained expression and had obviously not been to bed that night because he was still fully dressed in his lab coat and was wearing outdoor shoes.

'It seems to be worse than last night,' he said gloomily. 'The pain, I mean. You're quite right, Flo — being walked through certainly does seem to do something quite serious. When I was younger it didn't seem to matter but now, well, it's got me very badly in the right shoulder and my back's very painful.'

'That's it then.' With sudden resolution Florence climbed out of bed and put on her cashmere coat. 'Get up, Frederick darling,' she said.

Frederick was still lying on the bed with the silk eiderdown pulled over his eyes. The moonlight was very bright that night and shone exquisitely through the little leadlight casements. He groaned faintly, then got up too. He quickly put on his camel-coloured trenchcoat and tied a tartan scarf around his neck. 'What a bit of luck ghosts don't have to change into pyjamas or the trousers might show under my coat, Florence,' he said, 'but I'm not altogether sure I look tidy enough.'

'Of course you do, darling, and you must remember, Frederick, most people can't see us at all and Mr McLeod will understand perfectly that it's a medical emergency and we've had to set off as we are. Come along, Claude. I cannot bear your pain any more. We're going down town to see Mr McLeod about your injuries. Frederick, you just nip along the hall, dear, and call Eddie. He'll want to come too, I feel sure. He might like to get Mr McLeod to have a look at his neck while we're there. Hasn't he said his neck's been a bit painful lately?'

Frederick plodded quietly away and within moments Eduardo had appeared in the bedroom doorway fully dressed in his better green corduroy trousers and his Harris tweed jacket with the leather patches on the elbows. He was wearing a burgundy paisley cravat and was fastening his best gold watch on his left wrist.

'We may need to know the time,' he said. 'As you all know, we must be home by the first crack of dawn or —'

'Quite so, quite so.' Frederick spoke hastily as if suddenly afraid. It would not do for them to be caught by the first rays of the dawning sun. At the very least it could ruin their eyesight.

'I had a feeling this might happen,' said Eduardo, 'so I lay down fully dressed and I've just been dozing. I felt that Claude might get worse in the night and we might have to go down and see old McLeod. I might ask him about my neck. It just seems a bit stiff some ways I turn. Maybe he could just manipulate it a bit and it might come right. Anyway,' he said, 'off we go.'

He sounded quite jocular, Florence thought, but as they so seldom left the property or even the house this was understandable. It was a sign of Claude's pain and fright that he had made no protest at all about going to see the chiropractor. Usually argumentative, he came down the stairs in a very docile way and walked miserably down the gravel drive with them to the gate.

'As I've already said dozens of times,' said Frederick apologetically as they all loitered for a moment by the letter box, 'I'd gladly take you in the car, Claude my boy, but my licence has lapsed and I think, under the circumstances, we'd get down to the surgery more discreetly if we just walked quietly down the hill together.'

'Perhaps hand in hand?' Florence put in nervously. She had always been frightened of the dark. 'I know the moon's shining beautifully, darling, but the shadows look very black, don't they?' She peered fearfully into some bushes by the gate because a snuffling noise seemed to be coming from in there somewhere. A hedgehog appeared slowly and waddled away in the moonlight after giving them a piercing glance.

'Isn't it lucky that animals can't speak,' said Frederick, 'or otherwise they'd tell a tale or two on us wouldn't they, my dear?' He tucked Florence's little gloved hand under his left elbow and they opened the gate to set off down the road. All the houses were in darkness except one and at its kitchen window they saw the hunched figure of someone drinking a cup of tea.

'Can't sleep,' said Eduardo kindly. 'Poor sod. I know how he feels. If you find the walk too much,' he said to Claude, 'just say the word and Frederick and I can link hands and make a fireman's lift for you. We can kind of carry you down the hill if we need to.'

'I think I'll be okay.' Claude continued to walk miserably down the middle of the empty road.

'My goodness,' said Florence as they rounded the first bend, 'how long is it since I walked down town?'

'Maybe ten years.' Claude was plodding along beside them with his shoulder held stiffly.

'Perhaps twenty.'

They walked along for another half a block before anyone spoke again and then it was Frederick who broke the silence.

'I do hope,' he said, 'that when we get back home — well, you know.'

'Indeed,' said Eduardo meaningfully.

There had been a terrible row going on earlier in the evening between Moira and Kevin Crumlatch, yet again about the house being sold. Perhaps the old row of earlier in the day had never satisfactorily ceased and they had just resumed the stream of insults and tears. Frederick, wincing, had blocked his ears and Florence had cried a few gentle little tears into her best lace handkerchief. 'That we should have come to this,' she had whispered to Claude as they huddled on the stairs like frightened children.

'I tell you, Moira,' Kevin had shouted from the upstairs bathroom, 'what I'm looking to do here is double my money.'

'Our money.' Moira had appeared with gentle inexorability in the bathroom doorway. She was wearing purple artificial satin pyjamas with the left leg ripped sideways below the knee. One button was missing from the jacket and the cuffs of both sleeves were deeply frayed.

Kevin had continued as if he had not heard or even seen her. 'So we invest two hundred grand in the old dump' — Florence had winced visibly — 'and we spend a bit here and there. So, at a conservative estimate, we've spread a few thousand around the place. All that rubbish and old sheds and stuff in the ghastly garden cleared away' — a groan had come from Claude at that — 'and new curtains instead of those filthy old velvet rags hanging at the windows.'

Florence had bridled prettily and Frederick had patted her knee. 'Dear one,' he had whispered to her, 'take no notice of the barbarian. He wouldn't know French antique silk velvet if he fell over it.'

'So here we are with a house we need to get four hundred thousand for and we're ready and waiting for it. We're ready and willing to make a real estate killing.'

'I'm not,' Moira had murmured, her voice muffled by a paper tissue in a luminous shade of violet. She had been weeping copiously into it and the colour had begun to run on to her thin cheeks.

'Does the woman never do anything right?' Eduardo had said crossly. 'Can't she even blow her nose on a paper hand-kerchief without creating a mess from here to the end of the world?'

'Ssshhh,' Claude had said. 'I'm listening. And don't be so intolerant, Eddie. She can't help it. She's just a clumsy old cow who's never had a chance. I mean, you'd think that bastard would buy her a decent pair of pyjamas, wouldn't you, and not polyester satin either — pure silk, at the very least, I'd think, on his income. But no — there she is in rags.'

'I do feel,' Florence had murmured to Frederick as she wiped her own eyes delicately with a scrap of hand-stitched cambric, 'that Moira and I have a few things in common. We usually cry at the same time.'

'I want to stay here,' Moira had said. 'I like living here. I feel I'm surrounded by friends.'

Florence dropped the handkerchief in sudden shock. 'Frederick,' she had said, 'do you think Moira might be more sensitive than we ever imagined? Might she possibly sense that we're here?'

It was at that stage that Kevin Crumlatch had slammed off to make a few business calls from his cellphone out in the garden and Moira, and the ghosts, had begun to prepare to go to bed but not to sleep. But the vibrations of all this earlier bitterness and misery seemed to drop away as the ghosts made their way down the big hill towards the town. The street lights shone down on a scene of great calm, just a few cats sitting on the pavement here and there and once a large woolly friendly dog padded up to them and licked Claude's hand. The gardens were full of flowers, the scent of geraniums and evening primroses almost overpowering. The spreading branches of magnolia trees provided dark mysteries on the boundaries of the larger properties and roses that were deep red in daytime lay blackly against white garden walls.

'This is really beautiful,' said Frederick. 'Maybe we should make a greater effort and get out more like this. I hadn't ever thought of taking a constitutional at night but sometimes it pays to have a different view of things and prioritise laterally.' He had been reading some of Moira Crumlatch's self-motivational literature which she often left lying about the house.

'I do agree. We should come out walking more often,' said Florence, taking Claude's hand for the last block.

Ahead, on the corner of Walter Street, they could see the old chiropractic surgery brilliantly lit by the moon and even though it had been taken over by a new man called Dr Chun since Alexander McLeod had died they knew they would find the original owner there, fully in charge of all his own instruments. Like Frederick's 1937 Chevrolet they would be superimposed over the new equipment, and the ghosts all quickened their steps to get there sooner. Suddenly it seemed a wonderful thing that they were to see an old friend after all this time in their isolated spectral states and even Claude, in pain though he was, took on a more cheerful aspect.

'I do think I might get Alexander to take a look at my neck,' said Eduardo thoughtfully as they knocked on the downstairs door that led to the big oak staircase with its old leadlight windows and copper lantern. 'He used to do me a lot of good when —' He stopped there. He had been going to say, 'When I was alive and had a bad neck.'

'When you needed it,' corrected Florence, smiling kindly at them all.

'Indeed yes.' Eddie felt relieved that Florence had put it so diplomatically. They all, by tacit understanding, preferred to be a little vague about the specificities of their lives and deaths.

If they had known anything about the warmth of their welcome they might easily have walked down the road months earlier. As they approached the intersection there was a loud exclamation of delight from above. Alexander McLeod was standing at one of the upstairs windows of the surgery waving violently. In a moment the window opened and he shouted down to them, 'How wonderful to see you all — come on up immediately. I'll put the kettle on.' They passed through the locked and bolted doors of the surgery as he ran down the stairs to greet them. A new security system had been installed with coded numbers but they took no notice of this. Alexander McLeod held up his hand in a small gesture of authority and they halted a few steps before the first landing where he had come to greet them.

'Don't tell me,' he said smiling broadly. 'Let me guess.' They all stood silently while he gave each one a searching glance.

'My dear Florence,' he said at last, 'how wonderful to see you. I see you're having a slight problem with that left elbow again. I should be able to fix that with a little manipulation. You should have come to see me sooner but I can very well understand your reluctance to venture out into the rude and vulgar world. I seldom go out myself these days.' He gazed thoughtfully at Frederick. 'Fit as a fiddle, I see,' he said, 'as usual, but maybe I could just give you a short massage of the neck area and perhaps a slight examination of the upper back might expose a little tension, but nothing to worry about there. But,' and here he looked searchingly at Claude, 'here we have what I would call a major problem. Claude, my dear boy —'

'I do wish,' said Claude rather petulantly, 'that people wouldn't always call me "my dear boy". I'm older than any of you, really, and I've been a ghost longer than anyone in the entire house and mostly in the street as well.'

'Sorry,' said Mr McLeod, clearing his throat and continuing in a more apologetic tone. 'Claude,' he said, 'I can see from your slightly twisted posture that you're feeling quite a lot of pain in the left scapula. I would say, and I'm only hazarding a guess here, that someone has walked through you and has almost dislocated your left shoulder blade, causing tearing of the nerves and a painful interlude prior to healing of the wounded tissue. Am I right?'

Claude nodded sulkily. 'It was that bastard Kevin Crumlatch,' he muttered. 'He got me really riled up the other day the way he was talking to Moira about selling the house and fleecing Lydia. I just stood in front of him to frighten him to death and —'

'Don't tell me,' said Alexander McLeod. 'Just let me guess. He walked straight through you? Right?'

'He got right up my nose.' Claude kicked the carpet miserably. 'I know Florence has told me not to have him on and let him walk through me, so it's all my own fault really. But it's just too much for anyone to take, the way he goes on. If he hadn't dismantled the garden shed it might be different. I could go down there and rattle the sheets of iron on the roof and have a good time —'

'I know, Claude. I know.' Mr McLeod spoke with a wealth of sadness hidden behind his cheerful words. 'We all find it very difficult to cope with things the way they are and not the way we remember. I must confess that I misbehave myself here upon occasions. Yes, yes, I do.' Florence and Frederick made demurring noises and Eduardo, who had had a long history of back trouble in real life and knew Mr McLeod well when they were all alive, actually shouted quite loudly, 'Oh no, no, never,' and a few remarks of that sort.

'Thank you,' said Mr McLeod. 'Thank you one and all.' He spoke with simple dignity and Florence got her best hand-kerchief out of a hidden inner pocket in her coat and wiped her eyes, which had suddenly filled again with tears of emotion. 'I must confess — and it is a relief to do so because it has been on my conscience for quite a time — that I've got seriously fed up with the swine who bought my old surgery and has got himself all set up here magnificently with computers and God knows what. He's such a little toad. You've really got no idea how hideous it is hanging around here all day invisibly and listening to him put me down all the time. It's "Mr McLeod didn't ever venture into computers", "Mr McLeod didn't have muscle assessment equipment like this", "Mr McLeod didn't have a website on the Internet," and that's just the beginning.' He gestured them up the stairs. 'Anyway, whatever can I be thinking of to keep you talking down here on the stairs in all these draughts. Do come on up to the surgery. I've got all night. You can have my full attention for hours, till at least cock crow. I'll put the kettle on and then we can go into all the medical problems properly. It's so wonderful to see you. Just wonderful,' he said with a slight catch in his voice.

Florence got out her hanky again and wiped her eyes. 'Frederick,' she whispered, 'we should have come down to see poor Mr McLeod sooner. I never realised other ghosts were as lonely and isolated as we are, though at least we've got each other. Poor Mr McLeod has no one at all. His nurse was quite a good soul but she's still alive and working for that doctor out at the port, and his wife was rather a loud, social kind of creature. She hasn't died yet either and I think I did hear on the grapevine that she married again, some plumber with big ears and a lot of money but no taste. Poor Mr McLeod has had a sad life,' she whispered as they climbed the stairs. 'Perhaps we should ask him up sometime. We could give a musical evening one night when the Crumlatchs are out.'

'Something should be possible, dear,' said Frederick. 'Never fear. The idea's in the pipeline now and I feel sure something will come of it. Maybe we should be more sociable. It's just a thing I've never really thought of in any detail.'

Alexander McLeod was rustling around looking for the spectre of his old tin of wholemeal digestive biscuits. At last he found it at the back of the cupboard. 'Claude,' he said as he poured the tea from his antique red enamel teapot, 'to cheer you up I should tell you that I have often let that awful fellow Chun walk through me on the days here when I've got in such a rage. It's ego of course,' he said reflectively as he passed them the milk and sugar, 'pure ego. I hoped I'd shock him into leaving but it did not a grain of good. As a ghost I thought I might be immensely frightening standing in front of him and having to be walked through. Not a bit of it,' he said bitterly. 'He's so caught up with his own monstrous ego he never even saw me or felt a thing. Lucky for me I've had in-depth training in how to withstand damage to the heavily boned areas of the body. You, Claude, have not been so fortunate, but I shall be able to fix you up, never fear. I do think, though, it might be best if you remained here for twenty-four hours in my old hospital room under complete observation.' There was a long silence at this disclosure. 'And you can play Scrabble with me and help me with the crossword in the newspaper.'

Florence nudged Frederick with her good elbow and kicked Claude lightly under the table. 'Of course,' she said, 'if you think it best that Claude should stay in your hospital he'll just have to stay. And we can easily walk down the hill again tomorrow night to collect him.'

'No trouble at all,' echoed Eduardo stoutly. 'It would be a real pleasure to see you again. I feel the outing has done us all good.'

The moon was waning as they walked home again, Eduardo just a little ahead of Frederick and Florence.

'I do hope Claude will be all right,' said Florence anxiously as she took Frederick's arm for the very steep part of the hill that led up to the old house. 'I remember this part of the road very well,' she said, giving his elbow a fond squeeze. 'This is where you always used to change down to second gear on that last big bend. Frederick, it does seem a long time ago that we had that dear old life and went to town every Tuesday in the Chevrolet.' Her voice contained a faint hint of a sob again.

'Never mind, Florence,' Eduardo said, 'we're all together and that's the main thing. You and Frederick are together and Claude and I are very lucky to be in the old house with you. I do worry about Lydia, though. After the stockmarket crash when everything was so terrible for her and she went away it just left me in a kind of emotional limbo, really. I do wish I knew how she is and where she might be. If only I could just see her again — even if she didn't know I was here. Of course,' he said reflectively, stopping in the moonlight for a moment so that Frederick and Florence nearly bumped into him, 'if I did see her she definitely couldn't see me. But' — he brightened a little — 'never mind about that. At least I'd know she was all right and I could make things easier for her in lots of little ways. I could make sure draughts didn't make her catch cold and that dogs didn't rush out from gateways to bite her and lots of little jobs like that. I could make things a whole lot easier for her if only she were nearby somewhere.'

He trudged along quietly for another half a block. All the houses were in darkness now, everything silent and still, and all insomniacs finally asleep. 'And if she went out on to the old portico to read the morning paper like she used to, I could make sure none of the pages blew away if she put them down on the garden table. Not,' he said rather bitterly, 'that there's a garden table there any more since that bastard Crumlatch turned the conservatory into what he calls an office and put some kind of computer in there and not that Lydia could read the paper there because she no longer owns the house. It really makes me sick. The whole thing makes me sick.'

'There, there, Eddie.' Florence patted his arm and whispered to Frederick, 'Darling, why don't you get out the spectral spectacles and just see if we could possibly get the tiniest glimpse of Lydia? It might be different outside. You might get a better beam on things or the air might be clearer out here. You've only ever tried to find her indoors. Why not put the spectral spectacles on and see if you can get any kind of glimpse of her, just to make Eddie happy, sweetheart?'

Much later, when they all related what they saw when Frederick got the glasses out of his special inner pocket they all told it slightly differently. Frederick said he was the first one to see the vision of Lydia curled up on what looked like a bus seat. Eduardo claimed he was the first to recognise the turn of her head even though her face was not, then, visible. Florence said she recognised the sound of Lydia's voice even before she heard it properly.

'There seems to be some kind of crowd, or group, of people and it looks as if they're on a bus, a double-decker bus. My goodness me, I'm suddenly getting quite a good view of something here.' Frederick was looking through the glasses and Florence and Eduardo were jumping up and down beside him, asking to have a turn. 'I've told you both before,' said Frederick patiently, 'that only one person can look after the spectacles and wear them officially. You can both have a turn in a moment but you'll have to wait till I've got them adjusted. This is such a surprise, such a shock. We've looked through the spectacles dozens of times and never seen Lydia. We've just caught darkness and mistiness which denote that she was a long way away. Perhaps' — he was fiddling with the lenses now — 'she is somehow on this bus I can see and maybe the bus is travelling towards us and this would account for our being able to see her. I'm getting a faint sense of remembered movement here as if the bus might have been travelling during the day but has now stopped and will start again tomorrow. According to the instruction book, the glasses can recollect the past and also foretell the future.'

'Good God,' exclaimed Eduardo vehemently, 'why didn't I ever know this before? Why wasn't I ever told this before?'

'I just forgot,' said Frederick lamely. 'I'm not really a very mechanical person and it slipped my mind.'

'Do you really think she could be journeying towards us?' Eddie's voice contained a world of hope. 'If not exactly now, then perhaps in the morning? How wonderful.'

'Perhaps,' said Frederick austerely. 'I'm not sure.' He was secretly illuminated by the idea that Lydia might be close to them but, equally, devastated by the thought that she would not be coming to the house because it was now owned by the Crumlatchs. And how would it be possible to make Eddie accept this horrible reality without spoiling his delight?

'Please give me a turn,' said Eduardo and his voice contained such a note of extreme desperation that Frederick handed over the glasses immediately. Eduardo had, after all, been fifty-eight when he had his sudden heart attack and died, so he must be adult enough to take life's vicissitudes, even though he had been a ghost for a shorter time than anyone else in the house.

'When you've had your turn,' said Florence in her clear, firm voice, 'can I have a look? I'd love to see Lydia again, even if it's only from a great distance. I always remember how nicely she had everything arranged in the house and I just loved that beautiful walnut table she put in the hall and all those lovely big bunches of garden flowers she used to arrange on it.'

When they arrived home they sat on the stairs till dawn in their usual positions to discuss the momentous events of the evening and take turns with the spectacles; each time the vision of Lydia grew clearer.

'She's definitely been travelling towards us,' said Frederick, his voice slightly muffled within the folds of the collar of his best overcoat which he had worn down to the chiropractor's surgery and had not yet taken off. 'I didn't know there were double-decker buses here but I suppose things have changed since —'

Eduardo rescued him kindly. 'We're country people,' he said blandly, 'and there must be a lot about life in the city that we haven't ever kept up with.'

'Indeed,' said Frederick his eyes glued to the lenses. Mrs Jackson had come into view. 'There seems to be quite an elderly woman, very smartly dressed, limping up and down the bus having a word with people. Maybe she's some kind of hostess. I'm a trifle bewildered because it seems to be daylight in this view I'm getting but perhaps it's a recollection of yesterday.'

'It's so difficult being a ghost,' sighed Eduardo. 'I bet people who're still alive don't have to worry about seeing all the time zones at the same time. No wonder we get headaches and scream a bit at midnight.'

'How right you are,' said gentle little Florence. 'I remember years ago when I sometimes had to catch a bus I often felt quite nervous that I might have got on the wrong one by mistake. It might have been nice if there were a hostess I could have asked about it. Modern life must really be quite kind, mustn't it, if they have hostesses on buses.'

'She seems to be wearing rather an impractical pair of blue velvet high-heeled mules trimmed with rhinestones and feathers,' said Frederick enigmatically, 'and also a very low-cut frock like we used to see in Hollywood movies with Joan Crawford.'

'How exciting,' said Florence innocently. 'Perhaps she's just unbuttoned her top a little bit because it could be warm on the bus and perhaps they don't want to open the windows in case mosquitoes fly in and bite people. What else can you see, dear heart?'

'Well, there seems to be a very tall girl dressed in what looks like a kind of brief tiger-skin drape and she's covered with tattoos, and Lydia's been walking up and down the bus with her having a chat to various people. She seems to know the woman in the rhinestone-trimmed mules, and the tall girl in the animal skin outfit is handing her a paper handkerchief, as I speak.'

'Perhaps they're friends of Lydia's,' said Florence kindly, 'and maybe they're all in fancy dress because they're coming to a party or something like that, do you think, Frederick?'

Frederick said he didn't know.

'Oh well,' said Florence, 'I think it might be best if we all snatched an hour or two of rest and awaited developments when day dawns. If Lydia is coming to this part of the country I feel certain she must come up here to see her old house. Perhaps she'll bring all her friends with her. What do you think Lydia's wearing, by the way? It looks to me like an evening dress.'

'Or a nightie,' said Frederick, again enigmatically. 'Something Grecian anyway, and very pretty. It seems rather an odd garment to travel in but fashions have probably changed in recent years. Lydia always had a unique fashion sense and her own look.'

'It's just so wonderful to see her again.' Eduardo, quite overcome with emotion, sat on the bottom stair, smiling broadly and laughing wildly in excitement. 'If she comes up here to see the old house we can expect her later in the morning, I suppose. Perhaps we should all snatch some rest if we can, just so we look our best to see her.'

'His depression seems to have lifted remarkably,' said Frederick as he and Florence watched Eddie almost run up the stairs, shouting gladly.

The door of the master bedroom opened suddenly and they froze immediately. 'Moira,' said Kevin in a very irritated tone, 'I think we've got rats. There seems to be a helluva row coming from out here — scampering and what sounds like voices squeaking and heaven knows what. You'll have to go and get some of those blue rodent pellets in the morning. We'll have to lay poisoned bait on the stairs at night.' From inside the room came a series of snores.

'What a hell of a life,' said Kevin sourly. 'A wife who snores and is about as appetising as a bowl of cold porridge, and now rats on the stairs. Is there no end to this shit? All I want to do is sell this house, double my money and get out of the place and I can't because no mug will come and buy it.'

CHAPTER
SEVEN

'I think it's time for some music,' said Frederick early the following morning. They were all still a little pale after their disturbed night and the excitement of their walk down the hill. Eduardo had lapsed into acute and desperate disappointment for a few minutes when it was discovered, as the town clock struck eight, that the spectral spectacles no longer showed the bus or Lydia or the mysterious elderly woman who was so brightly and unsuitably dressed.

'But there are hills, my boy,' said Frederick earnestly, taking his arm in sympathy, 'and many gorges and ravines in the last part of the journey here, as you may very well remember yourself if you think about it. The spectacles simply couldn't see through all that. What we really need is a clear view of the main road and I feel sure we may get that later in the day.'

'Do you really think so?' Eduardo asked, brightening a little. 'The main road was very difficult in parts, I do remember that.'

'We live in quite a precipitous part of the countryside,' said Florence carefully as she cast on enough stitches for the first sleeve of her favourite cardigan. 'Knit one, purl one,' she began to intone again quietly to herself. 'I don't think we'll be able to see Lydia again, or any of them, till much later in the day. Perhaps,' she said prevaricating wildly, 'not till they're nearly here.'

Frederick gave her a warning look. It would not do to get Eduardo's hopes up too high. They had woken very early and had already discussed in great detail how they would cope with Eduardo's excitement and then possible depression if the spectacles had somehow made an error. 'Maybe it was just an odd reflection,' Frederick had said quietly, 'or a trick of light, or anything. Are we, Florence, quite, quite sure it was Lydia we saw? Does it seem likely, in the harsh light of day, that Lydia would be wandering around the countryside in a double-decker bus, dressed in what looked like a nightie and with another woman in animal skins? And then there was that hostess wearing an unsuitably low-cut evening frock and high-heeled sandals trimmed with feathers.' He thought for a moment or two. 'And at her age, too,' he said. 'She looked all of sixty or seventy if she was a day.'

'Oh Frederick.' A few tears had crept down Florence's cheeks then. 'It does seem peculiar when you put it like that. You don't think we imagined it, do you? You don't really think Lydia's not anywhere near us after all? Oh Frederick, whatever will we do if it isn't true?'

'We must take refuge in music while we wait,' said Frederick stoutly. He and his beloved Florence had decided that their sudden doubts must be kept hidden from Eduardo. 'Dear old Beethoven will get us through the trials the day may hold,' he said. 'I think I'll just nip downstairs with some of this music I've had stowed away under the floorboards and we'll have a bit of a tune-up. Eddie, I'll need you to turn the pages.'

'Frederick,' said Florence admiringly, 'you're just so decisive it takes my breath away.'

Under the stairs, in what had once been called the violin room, a guest cloakroom had been installed with matching vanity and circular towel rails for lace-trimmed polyester guest towels in luminous colours. The spectre of the old pan-elled cupboard that had once held Frederick's violins was still there leaning mistily against the wall, which was now covered in plastic lining board.

'What a disgusting decorative mess,' said Eduardo bitterly as he sagged against the architrave of the entry door. It was all so depressing.

'Never mind about all that.' Frederick was rattling around in the old cupboard. 'The thing is, Eddie, do I want to play my Giovanni Maria Ceruti' — he waved a violin case he had drawn from the depths of the cupboard — 'made in Cremorna in 1923? It's not really a very old instrument but a good one, I hasten to add, and always a reliable tone. My darling Florence bought it for me on one of our trips to London. How well I remember the happy day we spent at Sotheby's while all the violins were being sold.'

He took it out of its case and dusted it lightly with a silk handkerchief that still remained there, tucked into the lining. He drew the bow lovingly over the strings, which had stayed in remarkably perfect spectral order. A few silver notes of the first violin part of Beethoven's Emperor Concerto wafted through the house. There was a sudden disturbance from upstairs and one of Moira's slippers flew past the small multi-faceted leadlight window of the old violin room and landed with a thud on the front portico.

'Cats again.' They could clearly hear Kevin Crumlatch's harsh voice echoing down the stairs. 'Moira, I'm going to buy an air rifle.'

Frederick, seemingly oblivious of this interruption, continued to play softly.

'Ah,' he sighed happily, his troubles forgotten. 'Allegro, allegro.' What a solace music is, Eddie,' he said as he put the violin back in its case. 'What did you think of the tone of that?'

'It seemed fine to me,' said Eduardo as he looked out the little window to see if the bus might be coming soon. Ridiculous, he thought. They could have stayed overnight somewhere to break the journey. It could be hours before Lydia arrived. The window was half open and he could smell the faint scent of violets and a tang of salt from the sea. Delicious, he thought.

'What about this one, though?' Frederick had drawn another violin case from the big cabinet and was opening it up. 'Now this is a very interesting instrument. This is my

Andreas Renisto,' he said proudly, 'an Italian violin made in 1927 so it isn't exactly ancient — not like a Strad or anything so exalted as that. But it's quite a good instrument. More expensive than the Ceruti, but that, of course, doesn't make it better intrinsically,' he added hastily as he began to play. He stopped after a minute or two and sighed faintly, then he, too, looked out the little window. Eduardo seemed cheerful enough this morning. It might be best to continue pretending to rehearse for a musical evening and hope for the best.

'Florence paid quite a bit for this one,' he said. 'Maybe nearly three thousand American, I think, if my memory serves me correctly. The Ceruti was a bit cheaper — maybe that could have been only sixteen, perhaps seventeen hundred American. I've just forgotten. She bought it for me for second best, if I had to play in a damp venue. They're both good instruments, though. I think someone from the Symphony Orchestra came and bought them at my sale,' he said mildly in the throwaway kind of tone that ghosts always use when speaking of their estate auctions. 'I actually went down to the sale,' Frederick said nonchalantly. 'You can sit up on the cross-beams and see who's buying what and how much they pay. It's quite good fun really, if you like that sort of thing.' He played another few bars experimentally. 'Of course it would sound a whole lot better if I had the whole orchestra with me as in yesteryear but that, sadly, I cannot conjure —'

'Look out,' shouted Eduardo, but by then it was too late. Within moments they were splattered vigorously with water from the garden hose.

'Gotcha,' they heard Kevin Crumlatch shout from outside the wall. 'Moira? Moira? You'll have to keep this cloakroom window shut all the time — the cats are getting in.'

'Really,' said Frederick in a very bored tone as he put the Renisto back in its case after drying it lightly with the silk handkerchief. 'Who does he think he is, I'd like to know.'

Later, in the garden, they continued the rehearsal. Eddie held the music up and Frederick sometimes followed it and sometimes extemporised, depending on his sudden mood swings.

'I say,' he said after half an hour or so, 'I do hope Kevin Crumlatch comes on a little poorly this evening. I had a kind of experiment with him as we left the house. I'm not sure you noticed, Eddie, but I walked through him. Now it's a moot point about who damages whom by walking through them. So far, I've stood in front of people to frighten them, and in the case of Kevin Crumlatch I've drawn a total blank, but I — and here I'm speaking as a spectral entity and not as an individual — have never walked through anyone. People have walked through me and made me ill, but I've never walked through anyone. I wonder how he'll feel as evening falls and the dew starts to appear on the ground.' Frederick always said this was a telling time of day. 'What do you think, Eddie?'

'Dunno,' said Eddie with uncharacteristic brevity. He was watching the area that led to the gate and his attention to everything else was perfunctory. There was still no sign of the double-decker bus.

'It's a shame all the people in my trio haven't died yet,' said Frederick after a few minutes of scales and arpeggios. His skill on the violin, even with so little practice, was remarkable. 'I understand Reuben Grimwade succumbed last year but, as you know, Eddie, Florence and I seldom venture out these days.' He sighed deeply. 'Reuben lived over in Southern Heights. I know it's just a few minutes' drive from here but, believe me, if you have to walk over there it's quite a step, what with the gully and everything.' He sighed again. 'I suppose poor Reuben's over there all on his own with no music or anything and not a soul to talk to. I understand his old house was sold very quickly to some people who did it all up and made it unrecognisable. They spent, so I hear, thirty thousand on the kitchen alone. Poor Reuben,' he said sadly. 'I haven't really thought of him a great deal and I feel I should have. I've been a neglectful friend, Eddie, and I feel ashamed.' He played a few more bars of something that Eduardo failed to recognise. 'That was the beginning of one of Reuben's own little compositions,' said Frederick softly and reverently. 'We used to play it sometimes as an encore in the great old days of the old trio.' He sounded close to tears.

'Perhaps, now we've started going out a bit, we could get in touch with him somehow.' Eduardo was still staring towards the gate.

'What a good idea,' said Frederick. He played a few more bars of something largo assai de expressivo. 'Just another musical scrap from my mind,' he said in a thoughtful tone. 'It all seems to be coming back to me now. It could be quite a good idea for us to get back into the habit of having the odd musical evening. It's a matter of making contact with people. I feel sure they would be pleased to mingle — that's the term they use nowadays, isn't it? Mingling?' He suddenly gave a brilliant smile. 'I know,' he cried, 'I know. We could have our little concerts, if they could be arranged, at Alexander McLeod's surgery. No one would hear us and there'd be no complaints.'

'Nothing like the hose just now,' said Eddie with a twisted but humorous smile.

'Indeed not.' Frederick spoke feelingly. 'One could play away endlessly, to one's heart's content, and no one would ever hear — except us, of course,' he added hastily. 'There'd be us. But it would be as quiet as the grave down there and we could do whatever we liked without anyone complaining or interrupting.'

'Maybe we could telephone Reuben?' Eduardo was still looking fixedly towards the gate. 'Do people like us use the telephone?'

'I haven't heard of it,' said Frederick. 'Mrs Huddlestone, on the few occasions I've seen her recently — and by that I mean the last ten years — has never said she uses the telephone. Perhaps' — and he lingered over the words painfully — 'we aren't supposed to use it, do you think? Perhaps it's part of the real world and we're barred from it?'

'There's always Mrs Huddlestone's bicycle,' said Eduardo stoutly. He was extremely fond of Frederick and hated to see him upset. 'If Mrs Huddlestone can still correctly ride her bicycle, within the parameters of what we're allowed to do, well I see no problem with my borrowing it and biking over to give a message to your friend Reuben some night. And if I can't go, Claude, I feel sure, would love to.'

'Beverley Wylie, our very able pianist, is still alive,' said Frederick with a sigh, 'so we couldn't have a trio like we used to, but Reuben and I could play duets. Beverley,' he said, 'was a wonderful woman. Heaven knows why she remained here all her life. If only she had gone to Paris or New York or Berlin or anywhere to study she might have made it on the international circuit, but she stayed here to look after her mother.' He sat down slowly on the lawn that Kevin Crumlatch had mowed right down to stumps of grass through which the parched earth showed dully. 'I don't think we should take the Crumlatch cruelty too personally,' he said after a moment or two, pointing to a dying clump of grass, 'he's even nasty to the poor old lawn and it was so verdant in our days here.'

Eduardo coughed nervously. It would not do to let Frederick lapse into depression about the state of the garden, which was now pruned and clipped right back to the bone. The old wild swathes of daisies and violets had long gone, and the scrambling luxury of the wisteria that had rampantly covered the old garden shed had been killed with Roundup from a hired sprayer during the Crumlatchs' first week in the house. The garden was deathly tidy.

'Tell me what Beverley Wylie was like as a pianist,' he said quickly, grasping at the first topic of conversation he could think of. He thought he remembered her vaguely in the town — a biggish woman, he thought, with beautiful reddish-blonde hair piled, French-style, artistically and wildly on top of her head and fastened with a comb made of Baltic amber.

'On anything andante she was very reliable,' said Frederick thoughtfully. 'Yes, excellent. Also andante cantabile, very good. But she was slightly unreliable on the runs and trills. I think she may have had the beginnings of arthritis in the knuckles of her left and right index fingers. There was a certain stiffness there which practice never cured, sadly. When we did, for instance, the dear old Emperor Concerto with the local orchestra the music critic said, with some justification, that she lagged behind a little in the quicker parts. But,' said Frederick, 'a good woman. A very excellent woman. Dedicated, dedicated. You don't get that now.' Yet again he seemed so suddenly steeped in nostalgia that Eduardo was concerned.

'Let's go back to the house and see Florence,' he suggested, rather wildly, and they both walked up through the beds where the roses had been viciously pruned back far too early so that their claw-like, truncated branches thrust desperately through the overtilled earth.

On the way Frederick waved his violin bow idly and whipped a few heads off the cinerarias flowering profusely in one or two darker corners of the lawn. 'Rather wicked of me,' he said to Eduardo as the flower heads flicked through the air, 'and not at all good for my dear old bow, of course.' He twirled it skittishly like a drum majorette's baton. 'But one really excellent thing about being —' and here he stopped suddenly.

Being a ghost, thought Eduardo wistfully. It seemed only a moment or two ago that he had been alive and he and Lydia used to dance on the lawn he and Frederick were walking over now. On summer evenings they used to play records on their stereo and, with the sitting-room windows wide open, the sound filtered beautifully out over the garden. How delicious it had been, he thought, to dance on the lush lawn with Lydia in his arms.

'The really excellent thing about being as we are,' said Frederick determinedly, 'is that we can misbehave like this and nothing comes of it because the real bow is miles away. I cannot harm it, no matter what I do.' He whipped off a few more heads and chuckled mischievously. 'I think someone, yet again from the Symphony Orchestra, bought it at my estate sale. Quite a charming lady violinist, I seem to recall,' he said, 'with very good legs. It was — or is — quite a pleasant little Arthur Bultitude — an odd name, isn't it, but he was quite a noted maker of violin bows in his own dedicated way. Yet again my darling Florence bought it for me on one of our trips to London.' His voice suddenly contained another sob and, as Eduardo watched, Frederick drew a handkerchief from his pocket and wiped his eyes. 'You must forgive me,' he said softly. 'I suddenly feel quite overcome.'

It seemed to be a quietly hysterical morning, Eduardo thought. Florence was exhausted and had sought rest in her Sheraton revival bed. Claude, in Mr McLeod's private ward, was probably also resting. Frederick, unusually, had suddenly seemed to become enmeshed in the musical world again. And Eduardo's inward excitement was so great he thought he could die if he had not done so already. It would be a momentous day, he thought. The sky was absolutely cloudless, a sparrow was bathing itself vigorously in the old birdbath by the front door, the droplets of water flying brilliantly into the clear summer air. He looked anxiously out through the remains of the magnolias and copper beeches to the road but there was still no sign of the bus coming.

'Frederick,' he said, 'do you think it might be wise, just in case that bastard Crumlatch has locked the gate, to check on whether Lydia could get in if indeed the bus does arrive?' He tried for a neutral tone but Frederick looked at him sharply.

'Eddie,' he said, and placed his hand on the younger man's shoulder, 'I do hope you're not getting your hopes up too much? I hate to tell you this but the spectral spectacles could possibly have picked up some mistaken vibration and it could all evaporate like the mists of time. Florence and I discussed this very question early this morning and although we're hoping for the best we're also expecting the worst, Eddie. I have to tell you the truth, sadly, and I'm very sorry. Florence and I are very sorry.'

'I know,' said Eddie stalwartly while believing in his heart quite the opposite. 'Thank you,' he said. 'I truly appreciate your concern, Frederick.' He tramped up through the garden to lift the latch on the gate.

CHAPTER EIGHT

Oswald was the only person at the Côte d'Azur who had ever seen where Mr Somerset-Smith lived. The year before last, in June, when a serious influenza epidemic struck the city, Charles Somerset-Smith had been taken home by Oswald as dawn broke on a fine but chilly Thursday.

They went in a taxi called by Richard Villetto himself on his own bespoke cellphone set on the upper side with cabochon rubies. And it was Mr Villetto who had said, as some of the girls clustered about, deeply concerned, 'You are certainly not going home alone, Mr Somerset-Smith. I would be most concerned if you did that. I must insist that Oswald goes with you to see that you're all right. I insist.'

As the vehicle drove through the empty streets Charles Somerset-Smith sometimes turned to Oswald and made the odd apologetic remark. 'Very good of you,' he said as the car went round the corner by Old Government House, and 'Most kind,' he murmured as the driver took the motorway turn.

He had arrived at the Côte d'Azur the previous evening looking flushed, his eyes too bright. Geraldine Jackson took him some of his favourite sandwiches, which he hardly touched. Lydia had propped him up against her lace-covered satin bolster and put a cool, damp cloth across his forehead. 'Mr Somerset-Smith,' she whispered in his ear as he lapsed into a troubled doze, 'I think you're not very well. Just lie quietly and I'll read to you. Mrs Jackson has brought you some fruit juice. Try to rest.'

'What a kind girl,' Mr Somerset-Smith muttered as the taxi left the motorway the following morning and travelled swiftly towards an area known in real estate as the Golden Mile. 'That one who read to me most of the night — what was her name again?'

'Lydia,' said Oswald. 'L-y-d-i-a.' Mr Somerset-Smith was slightly deaf.

'I must remember that.' Charles Somerset-Smith suddenly leaned forward. 'My gate is the second one ahead on the left,' he said to the driver. 'That one with the high gateposts and the stone lions on top. Yes, we're here — this one. Turn here, please.'

Later, back at the Côte d'Azur, Oswald silently, as if in a dream, went about his business of sweeping with his Provençal broom and attending to all the minor details of the day. Window-cleaning, dusting, calls to florists about exactly what sort of lily would suit the upper rooms, the dry-cleaning sorted and correctly labelled, discussions with Geraldine about the night's catering — he did it all automatically, his mind still on the events of the very early morning when the taxi crunched to a halt on the gravel drive in front of Charles Somerset-Smith's house.

They had driven through a shrubbery that had gone wild but still had the elements of a splendid garden design. The old rhododendrons had not been sprayed for lichen for a long time and many of the trees needed vigorous pruning. The drive leading to the house swept in a wide and generous half-circle, the edges covered with moss and dried leaves, and a waterless stone fountain in the middle of the front lawn thrust bleached stone fish and mermaids skywards as if making a mute appeal for rain.

'Problems with gardeners,' Mr Somerset-Smith remarked breathlessly as he climbed out of the taxi. 'The old place isn't what it used to be, sadly. In my father's time — well, never mind about that. No use dwelling on the past, Oswald. We live in the present, with all its horrors, and speaking of horrors here comes one now.'

A grim-faced woman came out through double front doors and stood at the top of the flight of steps that led up to the house. 'I didn't know whether to send out a search party or what,' she said sharply, arms akimbo. 'What sort of time is this to come home? And me with my muffins heated up and the kettle kept boiling half the night for your supper.'

'I've told you before,' said Mr Somerset-Smith as, wheezing, he climbed the steps with Oswald at his elbow, 'never wait up for me, Mrs Kirby. If I don't come home in one piece someone will find the bits in the park.' Oswald laughed slightly and the woman gave him a sharp look. 'If you'd just put the kettle on again and make a cup of tea for us, Mrs Kirby,' said Mr Somerset-Smith, 'my friend Oswald and I will have it in the library, thank you.' As Oswald stepped into a large entrance hall with a parquet floor stained black and white, he heard her footsteps echoing faintly in a corridor that must lead to the kitchen.

'Saddled with her, I'm afraid,' said Mr Somerset-Smith. 'Very difficult these days to find a decent housekeeper. I've never married. Therefore no wife. No sisters. Only child. Mother died in 1943. Aunts all dead. No one to keep house for me.' He was very breathless, his words coming in short rushes. 'Always meant to find a nice wife and settle down but kept leaving it till next year —'

'Perhaps it might be best not to talk,' said Oswald. The loud, unwilling tick of the grandfather clock beside an inner door was like the laborious beating of a heart about to stop.

'Better give me your arm, I think,' said Charles Somerset-Smith, and so together they went into a large room on the right.

'What shall we do about the taxi?' Oswald was becoming anxious about the car and its driver waiting outside.

'Don't worry about that.' said Mr Somerset-Smith airily. He waved an old veined hand that trembled slightly. 'They'll just put it on my account. They're used to me,' he said. 'I'll call them up again when you're leaving and they can send the same driver to take you back to my home away from home, the dear old Côte d'Azur.' His faded blue eyes held a faint twinkle so Oswald sat down in a large antique armchair covered in old rose pink silk. He was slightly reassured that Mr Somerset-Smith seemed not as ill as they had all imagined. 'I do love the Côte d'Azur,' said Mr Somerset-Smith, 'but you must know that. Since I retired from the bench I find I have few friends. Most of the people I used to know have passed on. One becomes more and more isolated. If it were not for you dear people — well, never mind about that. It's no good dwelling on life's problems. Ah,' he exclaimed as the large old hand-adzed door swung open again giving another glimpse of the shadowy depths of the entrance hall.

Was that a suit of armour in a niche over the other side? thought Oswald. Surely not, but the mullioned windows cast little light and the hall was full of mysterious shadows.

'I see you're looking at my life-size bronze of the celebrated Italian soldier Beniamino Alphonso Baptista,' said Mr Somerset-Smith, smiling brilliantly now. He loved people to recognise his acumen in the world of art, particularly in the realm of larger bronzes. 'One of my better buys of yesteryear. What an eye you've got,' he said. 'Not many people even notice it, let alone know what it is.'

Mrs Kirby was tramping dolefully into the room carrying a tray. 'If you don't do something about these wretched mats,' she said sourly, 'one of these days I'll trip over and break my neck.' She paused for a moment. 'And the clock needs winding.'

'Ah,' said Mr Somerset-Smith joyfully. He ignored her remark entirely. 'The tea. Thank you, Mrs Kirby. Just leave it here, please' — he pointed to a long stool in front of the marble fireplace — 'and my friend will pour, won't you, Oswald?'

'You're not related to Lee Harvey Oswald, are you?' said Mrs Kirby as she advanced reluctantly and suspiciously, 'because if you are I can't stay in the house.' The sourness of her expression increased as she regarded Oswald with distaste.

'Oswald is my Christian name,' murmured Oswald apologetically. 'My surname is —' But he got no further.

'That's all right then,' snapped Mrs Kirby.

'Sorry about that,' said Mr Somerset-Smith when Mrs Kirby had closed the door behind her and they heard her footsteps fading away through the house again. 'Her cooking's not so bad, but she wouldn't know a Persian rug if she saw one, poor soul. Her roast dinners are not unsplendid,' he said after a moment or two of reflection. 'Makes a jolly good gravy, but her rice pudding would glue you up for a month. No milk,' he said to Oswald who had tentatively placed his hand on the ornately worked pearwood handle of the significantly large late eighteenth-century Sheffield plate teapot, 'and one spoonful of sugar stirred anti-clockwise, thank you, Oswald.' He leaned forward with difficulty from the enveloping cushions of a large French armchair whose gilding was so ancient it had turned pale green. He took the cup of tea with a trembling hand. 'I see you also recognise the marvellous intrinsic and monetary worth of that teapot you are now handling so carefully. What a man of taste you are. By William Bingley, of course,' he said, 'Circa 1787, but you, of course, would know that already.' He spoke in a series of short gusts, owing to the shortness of his breath. 'It's been wonderful to talk to such a man of taste, Oswald. You cannot imagine how lonely it is to be called just a silly old man with a black teapot that needs polishing and a few old rags on the floor.'

Much later that day, as evening was falling and it was nearly time to go out and sweep again, Oswald confided only in Richard Villetto the full extent of the mysterious grandeur he had seen earlier in the day, though Mr Villetto let the news slip to Mrs Jackson.

To the girls he had been less voluble, even obfuscatory, certainly mysterious. 'What sort of time did you have? You were away for ages. Where does he live? What was it like? Where is his house? What did you do? Has he got a family? Who was there to look after him?' They had clustered around him in a throng, already dressed in their leathers ready for the evening's congress.

Oswald had, in the end, pressed his fingers to his ears and said, 'No more, please.' And then with dignity to match his . host's he had said, 'Mr Somerset-Smith has a very nice home, do be assured of that, and yes, there was someone to look after him, so don't worry. Everything was as it should be. As I left he was going upstairs to bed and his housekeeper was going to light a fire to air his room in case it might be even faintly damp. She actually felt she had been a little remiss not to have done so earlier. His bedroom has a very pretty little fireplace but they seldom have a fire upstairs because of the problems of taking wood up the stairs and so on. It's quite readily understandable. She seemed a very excellent lady and cooks wonderful roast dinners. Her rice puddings are a little stiff but, then, so are a lot of things.'

With these few enigmatic remarks the girls seemed satisfied and drifted off to their various special rooms for the evening. To Richard Villetto he was more forthcoming. 'It was classically stylish,' Oswald said thoughtfully, 'without being in any way fashionable. Difficult to explain such a place, really.'

Mr Villetto lit up one of his very infrequent cigars and sat back in his chair.

'Try me,' he said, and waited.

'There were all these big bay windows,' said Oswald, 'not fitted with windowseats but with furniture like I've never seen before. Chairs and sofas made of carved wood in a light colour, some of it gilded but gone very old and worn, and with upholstery in coloured silks, some of it very tattered —'

'Ah yes.' Richard Villetto stared thoughtfully into space for a moment or two. 'True style, Oswald,' he said. 'True style. Genuine French furniture. Probably the fabrics would be antique silk, and it would be a sacrilege to replace them. This is the really genuine stuff, Oswald, not like much of the furniture I have here which is, very sadly, mostly just the better type of reproduction for which I have been seriously done in the eye.' He sighed sadly. 'What else, Ossie?'

Oswald was silent for a moment or two. Richard Villetto had only ever called him Ossie twice. The first time was when the wife of a well-known industrialist who had been recently knighted sent him a one-carat diamond tiepin and a sweet little note written in mauve ink in which she said she hoped her new title would make no difference to their relationship at exactly 3.30 p.m. every Friday. Stained with what looked like tears, or possibly gin, the note ended, 'I hope, dear heart, you will always call me Elsie because I am no lady as you very well know. With fondest regards.'

'My word, you seem to have made a hit there, Ossie,' Mr Villetto had muttered as he got his jeweller's glass out to inspect the diamond. 'Flawless,' he had said as he handed it back, reluctantly. 'Maybe a trifle yellow, but let's not be too picky.'

The second time he called Oswald Ossie was when little Sebastiano, then aged nearly two, tottered to the edge of one of the spa baths and disappeared beneath its surface as the Côte d'Azur's annual Christmas party reached its climax with the arrival of Santa Claus and his large bag of toys in a golden Rolls Royce. Every eye except Oswald's was upon Santa. Oswald, who had no children and had nothing to expect in the way of gifts, was gazing about in a bored fashion. Even though he entirely lacked parental instincts he jumped straight into the water and dragged Sebastiano out before anyone realised what a near-tragedy there had been. This also ensured that the child's special handmade romper suit in finest cambric did not shrink too badly. Oswald's socks were ruined but they were only 35 per cent merino wool and the remainder polyester so he hardly liked to make a fuss.

'My heartfelt thanks, Ossie,' Richard Villetto had said, though they were hardly able to hear his voice because Ambrosia and Annunciata and Mrs Jackson and many of the girls all screamed so loudly at the thought of what might have happened.

'I thought there was a suit of armour in the entrance hall but you know what my eyesight's like these days. I think it was really some kind of large life-size bronze statue. Italian, I think. He did say the name of the person it was supposed to be of but I've forgotten what it was. Some kind of soldier, I think.'

'Never mind. I've got the picture,' said Richard Villetto. 'Were there by any chance no fitted carpets but just mats around the place — mainly red and blue, possibly very faded?'

'Quite so,' said Oswald, 'and the housekeeper, this Mrs Kirby I told you about earlier, well she seemed very annoyed about them. Complained about tripping over the fringes and so on.'

'Philistines, philistines,' said Mr Villetto. 'The world, Oswald, is full of them, sadly.'

'He did say she cooked a very nice roast dinner sometimes,' said Oswald. 'And the tea and toast she brought into the sitting room we were in — well, that was nice too, except the toast was very cold. It seemed to be miles from the kitchen. You could hear her footsteps echoing away down corridors, right out to the back of the place, I suppose. I helped him up the stairs. They were very wide and curving and there were three landings before we got to the top. Luckily on each landing there was one of those little sofa things, like the ones in the bay windows, so we could have a sit down. Funny thing, though. The only place there was a proper light was in the stairwell. There was a big lantern hanging there but all through the rest of the place were just these lights on the wall made of brass.'

'Ormolu,' said Mr Villetto wearily. 'I think what you're describing here is a sort of fin-de-siecle elegance that's rarely seen these days. You've been privileged, Ossie, privileged to see it.' He sat deep in thought for a few moments. 'And the old boy didn't seem to have any family, you say? Maybe we could invite him to our Christmas party. Maybe he could bring the housekeeper, too, if he wanted to. Did he have a dog? Maybe he could bring his dog if he's got one.'

'Dog?' said Oswald. 'I didn't see a dog anywhere. He seemed to be more interested in art.'

'Art,' said Richard Villetto. 'What do you mean — art?'

'Paintings,' said Oswald. 'He had this odd selection of big paintings all around the place. Up the stairs, in his bedroom, in the sitting room we were in, just everywhere, and the funny thing about them is that they were all nearly the same — just these kind of water lilies in some sort of biggish pond thing. Sometimes there was a bridge, sometimes not. Done at different times of day, I suppose. Some looked like daytime, others I thought were more twilight-ish. Mainly blue, or a lot of blue. Maybe some pink. Gold frames. That kind of stuff.'

'Oh my God, Ossie, oh my God, Ossie, oh my God, Ossie.'

'They looked quite dabby to me,' said Oswald, 'though I must say they were far from small. One good thing about them is that they seemed to cover a lot of wall.'

'You don't mean the walls were covered with Monets, surely?'

In the end Oswald ran to fetch Mrs Jackson. 'Mr Villetto's been taken poorly,' he said. 'Do come quickly. I don't know what to do. He just keeps repeating the same thing over and over again — something about money, I think. Perhaps we should send for the accountant.'

CHAPTER
NINE

A s Frederick was playing a few tender bars of his old friend's composition down in the garden many kilometres away to the north Richard Villetto was battling to get all the girls back on the bus.

When it had become apparent the previous evening that they were definitely not going to reach their destination that day he had decided the party would stay overnight at a large country hotel. He had not anticipated that so many people would converge upon the place in the evening nor that after dinner there would be a kind of impromptu ball at which Samsonette would star in her imitation leopard-skin draperies and all the girls, even Geraldine Jackson, would chip their nail polish so that a manicurist would have to be imported from the nearest town to repair the damage the following morning.

'Do not imagine,' Mrs Jackson had declaimed over the silver dish of grilled sausages on the buffet, 'that I am going to waft about the countryside in a state of disarray for anyone.' She waved a hand under his nose. 'My left hand is a total disaster,' she said. 'I shall have to have my nails done again. You' — and she almost poked him in the chest with a finger — 'will have to do something about it.'

'Yes, yes. All out otherwise.' That was Celine in declamatory mode, literally standing on a box — a beer crate — out in the hotel yard where the bus had been parked overnight. 'Hands up everyone whose nail varnish is chipped and who needs a professional manicure.' She sounded very much like a union delegate, thought Richard Villetto, even though her costume was so brief and very unsuitable for the slightly frosty morning. A sea of hands waved about. He groaned. It was going to be a far more arduous trip than he had ever imagined.

Yesterday, during the stop for ice creams, so many people had gathered, including the truck drivers, that it had been an embarrassment. He had already run out of professional cards enumerating the talents and delights of the Côte d'Azur and they had been away from home eighteen hours or so — five or six of those had been spent in sleep. He had had to tip the receptionist at the hotel heavily to get two hundred photocopies of the only card he had left. Unprecedented, he felt. Unexpected. It was giving him a headache. It was all too much.

Because of the dancing and the dinner and the motor-bike rides with young farmers up and down the road leading to the hotel, most of the girls had not retired till very late. Mrs Jackson, owing to her age, had not been asked if she wanted a ride but an elderly man who ran a large sheep station nearby had turned up with a vintage Bentley and Mrs Jackson had driven off in that with him, waving a hand vaguely out the window. She claimed now to have chipped her nail varnish on the car's walnut fascia.

'Something will have to be done,' she repeated now as they all stood outside in the hotel yard waiting for the mechanic to check the bus. There had been a problem with the carburettor late yesterday and he had also thought it best to fit new spark plugs and clean the points. There was a small service station beside the hotel and the sole mechanic had worked through the night.

'You'll be right now,' he called, wiping his hands on the front of his tartan shirt before placing an arm around Samsonette, but Richard Villetto was already on his cellphone dialling up a manicurist from the nearest town. 'No extra charge for after-hours work as long as you give me a card,' said the mechanic. But Mr Villetto's attention was elsewhere.

'Do you have No. 46, a shade of pale lavender shot with pearl?' he was saying into the telephone. 'No?' He sighed deeply. 'Well, what about anything in the new line of pastels? Anything faintly mauve that's markedly pink and without much in the way of blue tonings. And not a very shiny finish — we like more of a matt, thank you. And nothing translucent because you lose such a lot of colour. Okay, okay. That might do. Just excuse me while I consult with my girls. Hands up everyone who might find it acceptable to have Nearly Nude as a base coat, then a second coat of Iced Coffee to intensify the colour range. Thank you, girls.' Most of them had put up their hands. 'Yes,' he said wearily into the cellphone. 'They seem to quite like that idea. If you could just make your way here as quickly as possible we might be able to get under way again by lunchtime.' A groan broke out from a group of young men who were milling around the bus talking to various girls.

'Why not stay to lunch?' one called. They were mostly wearing designer jeans, cashmere jerseys and highly polished riding boots. Putting on his reading glasses as nonchalantly as he could, Mr Villetto tried to decipher the name on the watch face of the nearest one. R-o-l-e-x, he read. The quality was unmistakable. He thawed a little. 'Perhaps just a quick sandwich,' he said. 'But nothing cooked. We really must get on our way.'

'Hurrah.'

Mr Villetto sighed again. It seemed to be virtually impossible to leave this place that he had thought last night was just a large old-fashioned hotel in the middle of nowhere. The crowd suddenly parted and the nose of the vintage Bentley appeared. The elderly farmer stepped out and presented Geraldine Jackson with a large bunch of country flowers including roses, daisies and several delphiniums. He, too, was wearing highly polished riding boots, a cashmere jersey and Dockers. The quality, thought Richard Villetto again, was eloquent.

'For you, dear lady,' the farmer said and joined the crowd. Mr Villetto stared fixedly at the man's watch — R-o-l-e-x, he read again and, startled, looked around. There certainly must be money in these green hills. He put his head in his hands. Perhaps they would never get away from the place, he thought despairingly.

Even Lydia was more cheerful this morning and had been for a ride up and down the road on a docile but beautiful roan mare brought up to the hotel by yet another farmer. He, unusually, was wearing a Versace tracksuit. Lydia was still looking like a more adult Ophelia in her chiffon nightdress with the blue velvet flowers in strategic parts of the draped bodice. Richard Villetto sighed deeply again. Perhaps they would have to stay there forever.

'I've got a very nice white mare I could bring back tomorrow — if you were going to be here,' said the farmer in Versace, 'otherwise I'd like one of those cards, thank you.' He had approached Mr Villetto confidentially. 'I usually sell my stock down south but I can easily change and go north so I could see her again. Always ride in a little Grecian dress, does she?' He shrugged one laconic shoulder slightly in Lydia's direction. 'Fine by me,' he said. 'Great. Loved the bare feet with the mauve pearly toenails.' He placed the photocopy of the Côte d'Azur's official card in his pocket with care and snapped the fastener shut sharply.

Richard Villetto looked at him assessingly. Perhaps a country branch, he thought, but how was this to be managed? He would need large and commodious premises, a staff of lovely girls, a trustworthy manager, decorators, domestic staff and so on. The amount of money involved could be ludicrously large. So there were not only the logistical difficulties of the day to contemplate but also the possible overextension of his financial resources if he decided to expand the business. So many problems, he thought as he felt a headache begin. So many problems.

Later, as the double-decker bus lumbered on its way through the small towns and farms that lined the main road, Richard Villetto felt a trifle more optimistic. It was, after all, only two in the afternoon. The light lunch provided by the hotel's management had indeed been the small sandwiches as he had stipulated. Served out on the wide and enveloping verandahs of the establishment it had been both casual and delicious, and some of the farmers had returned from the bar with ice buckets from which the tops of bottles of champagne protruded. He had felt a slight sense of disquiet about this but when he discreetly put his reading glasses on again he found the vintages were excellent. None of your Marque Vue or any of that awful pink lolly water, so no hangovers there, he thought hopefully as, tittering faintly, the girls climbed on the bus at last.

'Goodbye, goodbye, see you soon, love from me.' In a swirl of shouting and cheering the bus had left the hotel carpark with most of the girls waving out the windows. Even Lydia, he noted, had raised a hand in farewell as the man in the Versace tracksuit blew kisses.

Perhaps it was time to ring home again, he thought, so found his cellphone. 'Hello my darlink,' said Ambrosia throatily when she answered. 'Do not worry, my Mischka. All is vell here.' In the background he could hear Annunciata singing as Sebastiano played his flute. Ambrosia was obviously deeply enmeshed in watching old Ingrid Bergman movies on video again so that would keep her amused for a day or two. She always called him Mischka when she watched those. Her ultra, ultra latest bridge party and luncheon for all her friends must have gone off all right or she would be in hysterics by now. She was not missing him so he had a bit of leeway there. Excellent. He sat back in his seat and readjusted the cushions. Perhaps he might have just a tiny siesta.

'Excuse me, please.' That was Oswald doing the rounds of the bus with the Provençal broom. Some of the younger girls had been eating sugar-free sweets in paper wrappers and these were fluttering up and down the bus when it went round bends. 'Just a little bit of sweeping,' said Oswald.

'There you are,' he said, 'all immaculate again.' Disturbed, Richard Villetto gave a nameless kind of grunt and settled back in the seat. Oswald was really a bit much sometimes, he thought, with his cleanliness complex. He drifted slowly off to sleep.

At the front of the bus Oswald emptied all the sweepings into a special bag and sat down himself to ruminate again on that frosty morning when he took Charles Somerset-Smith home. What a pleasure that had been. Some of the trees along the route they were now travelling reminded him slightly of the magnificently overgrown avenue that led to the house. Copper beeches, oaks, silver birches — they had all been there in profusion. And there had been such a sense of camaraderie about it all. So endearing, he thought, closing his own eyes.

'I have often wondered if I should have married,' his host had said, after they had eaten their toast, leaning back in his chair and staring up at the crystal light fitting in a very thoughtful manner. 'An Edwardian chandelier,' he had said in a kind of aside. 'But of course you would know that, Oswald. I may call you Oswald? Thank you. And you, dear friend, must call me Charles.' He had settled back in the chair. 'Neo-classical,' he murmured and for a moment Oswald wondered what he meant. Ah, the chandelier, he thought. That would be it. 'Not wired up for electricity, of course, and we do not light the candles these days. Not in the front rank of designs, but a pleasant-enough little article.'

'Little?' echoed Oswald. The chandelier glimmered largely above him, set into a magnificently plastered recess of the coved ceiling.

'Little, relatively speaking,' said Charles. 'Some of them can be ten or eleven feet high. This is only seven, Oswald, but again, you would know that.'

Oswald made some kind of nameless murmuring noise.

'Such taste, such taste,' said Charles. 'It's such a pleasure to talk to you, Oswald. One has so very few kindred spirits in this harsh world of ours.'

'Mmmm,' said Oswald.

'And as for kindred spirits,' said Charles Somerset-Smith, sighing heavily. 'I have often wondered, Oswald, if it would have been wiser if I had, in fact, married. But who? This question perplexed and puzzled me for years.' He sighed heavily again. 'Until, at last,' he said sadly, 'it was too late. There was dear little Marion Crawshaw — I was very keen on her. We were childhood sweethearts. We won the mixed doubles at the tennis club way back — I forget when. I thought of her very seriously but at the end of some summer or another, just as I was going to speak, her engagement to a naval officer was announced.' He sighed heavily again and silence fell upon the room. 'He went down with the *Royal Oak*,' said Charles Somerset-Smith at last, 'and little Marion threw herself in the harbour. A sad day for me, a sad day.' The silence lengthened. 'If only I had spoken,' he said. 'If only I had written immediately, or even sent a telegram. But it's very awkward wondering what to do in a situation like that. I thought I'd leave it for a month or two and then send a large bouquet of orchids and follow it up with a delicate invitation to lunch at one of the better hotels. Maybe champagne, Oswald, served with caviar and Melba toast, followed by a light omelette stuffed daintily with mushrooms? I was going to take her shopping afterwards and buy her a diamond spray brooch as if it was absolutely nothing, just a mere bagatelle. I had it all planned, Oswald. I was going to tell her I had loved her for years but would wait till she felt she could consider me.'

'But you weren't to know what would happen.' Oswald, ensconced in the peculiarly comfortable and exquisitely gilded armchair beside the marble fireplace, felt greatly at a loss. Whatever could he possibly say in answer to all these confidences?

'Quite so, quite so,' Charles had said. 'And to further flummox me I had a vague acquaintance once who was deeply enamoured of a married woman. When her husband died he went to the funeral — miles and miles, Oswald, you couldn't imagine it, really. And it absolutely wrecked his car, fortunately a company vehicle, going through all that ghastly mud. After the funeral he approached the widow's son to make himself known and issue the odd tiny invitation to his hacienda for the loved one. All he said, Oswald, was that there was a bed for her at his place any time. He thought it may sound better coming, as it were, via the son. Result: nil. She never spoke to him again. Thought he was importunate, perhaps. Certainly too bold. What is one to do, Oswald? The son, he said, looked at him very coldly, indeed icily. And the widow wrote a freezing note to my old chum, just two lines, Oswald, that said, "The answer is no and no hope ever of any alteration. Yours sincerely, etcetera." My own delay in the same situation was caused by my horrible knowledge of that sad story and its even sadder outcome. I didn't wish to be too sudden, too quick about it. What else could I have done?

'Then,' said Charles Somerset-Smith, 'there was the beautiful Mildred Fosdyke. My word, Oswald, she made my old heart miss a beat or two and a few other things as well. Many a happy — nay ecstatic — moment have I had with my darling Mildred in the rhododendrons beside the club house at golf. Sadly, she too was unavailable.'

'But why?' Oswald almost shouted, his reaction totally involuntary. Surely Charles should grasp at happiness while he could?

'Sadly, my dear friend,' said Mr Somerset-Smith, 'she was married too and there seemed no hope of her husband becoming "the late", if you get my drift.'

'Could you have shot him?' said Oswald helpfully. He had once, for several years, been mixed up with gangs and violence was something he thought very natural.

'I would have liked to but unfortunately there are a few little things to do with the law that make shooting not what one would call viable, Oswald. If one were sure one would get away with it — well, then, it would be excellent. But' — he sighed heavily again — 'from my experience on the bench, Oswald, mostly people do not get away with shooting other people, even though the other people often deserve a bullet between the eyes.'

Oswald let a long silence elapse before speaking.

'Have you ever heard of hitmen?' he said carefully at last. Poor old Charles was so innocent.

'Indeed I have, Oswald,' said Mr Somerset-Smith and his faded blue eyes held a twinkle. 'And I have had many of them up before me for sentencing.'

'You seem to have a very big house here,' said Oswald, thinking it best to change the subject dramatically. 'How many rooms has it got, do you think?'

Mr Somerset-Smith stared at a carved marble caryatid that supported the mantelpiece. 'I cannot really tell you that,' he said, 'but I can say with complete authority that someone went off to count them one day and' — he paused dramatically — 'he never returned.'

'Never returned?' Oswald gave a gasp.

'No,' said Mr Somerset-Smith. 'No one ever saw him again, except from a distance. He met the chauffeur's daughter, who was a particularly exquisite creature, not unlike Lydia to look at though with nowhere near her brains and intellectual distinction, and stayed living in the chauffeur's flat for the rest of his life. When the chauffeur died he took over the driving. We just saw the back of his head.'

'I see,' said Oswald who was not sure he actually did.

'To get back to my bachelor status,' said Charles Somerset-Smith determinedly, 'there were a few others who took my eye over the years, Oswald, but I always left it till tomorrow or next week or next year to really reach a decision and then I'd look around and they'd be gone. One or two became nuns, some married. As time went by I noticed that many of those who had lingered for some reason or another were snapped up second time around. Widowers, you know, need a strong, fit, youngish woman to look after the house and mind the children without complaint and who better than some good-hearted but plain soul who thought she may never marry at all, Oswald? So they were all snatched from under my nose, often at the last possible moment.'

'Yes,' said Oswald who had no experience in such matters at all. 'Speaking for myself,' he said, 'I just had so many women at all hours of the day and night I never had the time to think of marriage. It would have been too much for me.' He sat sadly, steeped in thought about his old appointment diary that, each day, would be black with names and numbers. There was even a huge sub-list of people waiting for cancellations. 'I had my favourites,' he said 'but as far as I ever knew they were, in reality, unattainable. I just used to see them for half an hour or three-quarters of an hour on, say, a Wednesday afternoon or Tuesday morning or whatever, just when their husbands were away or at the office.'

'Really?' said Charles. 'You don't say.'

'There was one I was quite fond of personally, in my own odd way,' said Oswald. 'Her name was Angela and she was a frightful, cringe-making, boring old tart but terribly rich and paid anything you asked up front. There was just something about her that I found very intoxicating, even though she was as ugly as sin. It must have been a sort of personal chemistry or something like that. She was as dim as a doornail and had an awful voice like some kind of hooting foghorn in the lower registers or a screech when she hit the high spots. Pity is akin to love, so my old mother used to say. Maybe I just pitied her and thought it was the nearest thing to love I had ever attained.'

CHAPTER
TEN

After a late luncheon at 10 Fleming Street a domestic disturbance broke out again on various subjects. Kevin Crumlatch had a few things to say about Moira's mother, the sandwiches Moira had made yesterday, life in general, his hopes of making a lot of money out of the sale of the house, his foolishness in marrying Moira. 'When I could have done so well,' he said, sighing theatrically.

'How do you mean well?' Moira shouted through the kitchen door.

He had slammed it behind him and stood, as always, in the entrance hall for a moment or two. 'Well as in marrying Deirdre Weston-Smith, for instance.' He had placed his mouth close to the keyhole and a few bristles from his moustache caught in the keyhole. 'Ouch,' he said as he pulled them free.

'Ouch indeed.' Moira flung open the door. 'With her big feet walking all over you I bet you'd have said ouch.'

'How dare you speak of such a lovely girl like that.'

'She took a size ten shoe,' said Moira, 'and I should know because I worked in the shoe shop. And,' she said triumphantly, 'she was a triple B fitting, which means she had a foot like a dinnerplate.'

'You're a disgusting woman, Moira.'

'And you're a disgusting man.'

Florence, sitting on the stairs, sighed deeply. 'Do you think they'll finish soon, Frederick?' she said plaintively. 'I really can't stand all this. I mean, Freddie, our house was always a very peaceful place till they came here. Oh look. Isn't it awful. Now he's slapped her face.'

'I know, my dear.' Frederick patted her hand. 'Don't look. Don't distress yourself. Why not get your knitting out.'

'I might,' said Florence, and began to cast on the stitches for the second sleeve. 'I seem to be getting on quite well with it,' she said. 'I may finish it soon and then I can wear my favourite cardigan while you and Eddie have a little musical evening, perhaps.' She nodded her head conspiratorially up towards the head of the stairs. 'Have you seen what Eddie's doing?' she whispered.

'Indeed yes.' Frederick suddenly looked extremely concerned. Eduardo was sitting on the top stair with his head in his hands.

'Don't say he's going to have one of his fits of depression again,' whispered Florence. 'It's so terrible when he does that, even though it's not his fault. One feels so helpless.'

'We'll have another look through the spectacles,' said Frederick. 'Come on down, Eddie. Have another peek and see if she's in view.'

Eduardo came quickly down the stairs, put on the spectral glasses and looked for a long time towards the north. 'No,' he said at last, 'I can't see anything yet but I do see mist rising from the sea in one place and I see great hills and very deep ravines and she could easily be hidden somewhere in there. I wonder if she's still travelling on a bus or in a car. I suppose she might even be coming by aeroplane now, might she, for the last leg of the journey? In which case she could be thousands of feet in the air and none of us could see her till the aeroplane landed.'

'From my recollection of the matter,' said Frederick kindly, 'the road from the north doesn't really widen out till you're about thirty minutes out of town. She could easily be still on the bus and on her way and just not visible yet, as I said earlier. What about some music to pass the time?'

Eduardo murmured something noncommittal while Florence peered fearfully over the banisters. 'I'm trying to see what they're doing. Oh goody. Now she's hit him in the eye,' she said with satisfaction. 'I would not normally countenance violence but I do think he deserves it. The number of times I've seen him hit that poor woman. Now she's hitting him in the other eye. Now he's thrown the vase of flowers at the wall of the hall. Now he's slamming out the front door. Now he's gone. I think I can hear the car driving madly off.'

'Thank you, Florence, for that bulletin,' said Frederick who had sat with his eyes averted from the terrible scene. 'To think we all lived here so amicably, all of us, and since these people have been here there's been nothing but trouble.'

'At least the ghastly children have gone,' said Eduardo comfortably.

He sounded almost serene, thought Florence whose face puckered up at the thought of the Crumlatch offspring. There had been the daughter Sharon who had trained as a bus driver and mercifully driven off somewhere, and a drunken son called Jared who had thrown up regularly on the upstairs carpet. He was now training as a piemaker, fortunately at a distant bakery.

'Frightful,' said Frederick, his voice cracking with emotion. 'Just beyond belief.'

'We mustn't get too upset about the Crumlatchs,' said Florence who had picked up her knitting again, 'because we'll need all our energy for the rest of the day. I wonder, for instance, if we should go down to the surgery as soon as darkness falls to collect Claude or would it be better to wait till midnight, do you think?'

They began to discuss this animatedly and Eduardo placed the spectral spectacles on the sill of the stairwell window. If he had kept them on for a few seconds more he would have had a quick glimpse of the double-decker bus coming out of a deep gorge and taking a road that wound along beside the sea. Lydia was leaning against one of the windows in a state of gentle half-sleep and Celine, who was sitting beside her, was repairing her eye make-up. Then the vision faded as the bus went behind a series of steep hills and there was just the sound of great waves dashing on a stormy shore below the road. The spectral spectacles sometimes had a sonic quality in special weather conditions.

Eduardo, sitting on the stairs, put the glasses on again. 'Still nothing,' he said sadly and put them away in their special shagreen case.

Down in the entrance hall Moira was wiping her eyes with a large duster she had taken from the drawer of the sideboard. 'My life is a misery,' she shouted, 'just a misery.' She seemed to be looking straight at Frederick, who stirred a trifle uneasily.

'I say, Florence,' he whispered, 'you don't think she can see us, do you?'

'Definitely not.' Florence was knitting swiftly. She was halfway up the second sleeve already and had completed the back and one of the fronts of her favourite cardigan in the last two days. You could always gauge the stress of the household by how much knitting Florence got through in a day and her progress this week had been phenomenal.

'This marriage is at an end,' shouted Moira. 'I have had more than enough. I've taken as much as I can stand. I am at the stage of ultra ultra finito.'

'Up and at 'em, girl,' shouted Eduardo from the foot of the stairs. 'You tell 'em.'

'Ssshhh, Eddie,' said Florence. 'She might hear you, or sense the vibrations.' But she smiled quite brilliantly because it was so wonderful to see Eddie in good heart.

'I want a divorce,' shouted Moira. 'I want out. My life is just a hollow shell, just a lie, a complete emotional falsehood. My very presence at Kevin's side at the annual Christmas party for city retailers is a physical lie even though I don't utter a word. How can I, when that bastard talks all the time?'

'I do feel she's looking straight at me, Florence,' said Frederick in a low voice.

'Nonsense, dear. Knit one, purl one.' Florence had begun a rather difficult part of the pattern, a delicate cable that sometimes caused her a few problems.

'I'm going to see a lawyer —'

'Oh heavens,' said Eduardo, 'that'll cost the poor cow a fortune and it's my personal belief — correct me if I'm wrong — that it pays to stay away from lawyers. Once they get their hooks into you God knows where you'll end up. I knew of this lawyer once — what a bastard — slept with most of his women clients if they weren't too ugly and they never even had an —'

'Thank you, Eddie,' said Frederick in a reproving tone. 'I think something's happening down below. Just lean slightly to the right, will you please, so I can see?'

Moira, down in the entrance hall, was tearing off her apron and throwing it at the wall.

'My word,' said Eduardo, 'that poor wall's had a few things flung at it today.'

'Take that,' said Moira and threw her wedding ring as well. Then the ghosts had to hurry out of the way as she ran upstairs.

'She stood on my hand,' said Frederick in a very hurt voice. 'I usually have plenty of time to move. Moira's never usually deliberately cruel.'

'Here she comes again,' said Florence. 'We must try to find out what's happening.'

Moira ran down the stairs clutching her handbag and disappeared out the front door which she left wide open, swinging in a slight breeze. 'Let all his rubbishy furniture be stolen,' she shouted. 'See if I care.'

Eduardo looked fixedly down into the hall. 'I can see the ring,' he said, 'just glimmering faintly on the carpet.' He went downstairs, screwed up his eyes and stared intently. 'It's only rolled gold.' He had been reading the hallmark. 'Not even nine carat. Wouldn't you just know it,' he said sourly. 'When I married Lydia I bought her the best ring money could buy — eighteen-carat gold with an inlay of platinum all hand-worked by a noted goldsmith.'

'Of course you did.' Florence patted his knee comfortingly. 'And when Frederick married me he bought me the best too

— eighteen-carat gold set with a ruby. That was the style then. Poor Moira hasn't had much of a life, has she? No wonder she wants a divorce.'

'I want personal psychological enlargement' — they could hear Moira's voice fading away up the drive — 'I want to be happy and fulfilled, I want to be a real person, I want to believe in my abilities, I want to give up chocolate addiction, I want to be what I eat, I want to be ten kilograms lighter, I want . . .'

After a long and thoughtful silence Frederick at last spoke. 'Do you really think she's gone down town to see a lawyer?'

'Yes,' answered Eduardo and Florence simultaneously. They seemed overjoyed.

'And I hope she does him for every cent he's got,' said Florence.

'Florence!' Frederick looked extremely astonished. Never had he heard her speak in this manner.

'Sometimes, Frederick,' she said gently, 'I watch the same television programmes as Claude.'

Meanwhile, as the double-decker bus rumbled slowly southward Richard Villetto had awakened from his siesta. He judged they must have travelled a considerable distance. When he had closed his eyes they were deep in green rolling hills with large farms whose road boundaries were leafy with huge trees. Now the bus was trundling along in more brackish high country beside the sea which roared far below and dashed against eroded and uneven cliffs. The trees, sparse and skeletal, had been misshapen by endless gales from the ocean.

He closed his eyes again briefly and began to ponder various decorating problems he had with the Côte d'Azur. Was the art sufficiently expensive, avant garde and yet reassuringly in the masterpiece tradition to give the establishment the correct atmosphere, the right je ne sais quoi? Perhaps he needed to buy a few more paintings that depicted only women? This, sadly, might further enliven Celine about union issues.

As if motivated by his thoughts she came marching down the bus towards him. With her bright red hair put in a ponytail on top of her head and her deeply tattooed and amazingly long slim legs she was truly a daunting sight.

'Don't you think it's dreadful?' she whispered confidentially, nodding towards the crumpled figure of Lydia who was gazing soulfully out at the passing landscape. 'Fancy having to read in the newspaper that you lived in a place that was dirty. What a shock. And particularly when it wasn't true.'

'It wasn't quite that bad. The story just said the property was overgrown.'

'Overgrown? Overgrown?' Celine's voice could rise two or three octaves in a moment, thought Richard Villetto as he realised his error almost immediately. 'But overgrown means dirty and untidy and uncared for — all that kind of thing. The co-operative won't stand for one of its members being labelled publicly in such a way.' She flounced off up the bus again, her short chamois leather skirt swinging provocatively and the lustrous Parisian pearls that trimmed its pleats catching the light.

My word, temper or not, she was certainly an asset to his business, and the purple toenails were a masterstroke because they contrasted so deliciously and unusually with the impeccable bone structure of her slim tanned feet. She was really a splendid piece of human engineering, he thought before closing his eyes again to think of art. Maybe something slightly surreal, but very large and imposing. And all in gold frames, he thought. Definitely gold frames of the best sort. Real gold leaf, not the artificial stuff. Yes, yes. He would have to consult with some kind of expert. He drifted off to sleep again.

Back at the house in Fleming Street the atmosphere had lightened somewhat. Half an hour had passed since Moira went out the front door, allegedly to see a lawyer. Kevin had been absent for thirty-five minutes.

'Well, Frederick,' said Florence lightly, casting off the sleeve of her cardigan, 'what shall we do now?' This remark was really aimed at Eduardo who, once again, was sitting on the stairs with his head in his hands. The road outside the gates — she stood up to take tiny peek through the little leadlight window beside the front door — was still empty.

'Perhaps some music?' whispered Frederick, and Florence gave a slight nod. 'Eddie? Are you coming? Perhaps we could go into the sitting-room and you could strike the odd chord on the piano for me while I improvise a little, do you think?'

Eduardo stirred wearily. The day of waiting had been so long and there was still no sign of Lydia, not that she could even see him if she did arrive, he thought sadly. 'I'm not sure I have the heart for it,' he said at last. ' No, no. There's something on my mind that's been there for a long time — something I must say before this day is done. I do not think, in retrospect, that I treated Lydia properly.'

Florence dropped her knitting which rolled slowly down the stairs in a bundle. 'Don't say I've dropped any stitches,' she said as she went quickly down to retrieve it, 'Eddie, you mustn't give me a fright like that again. Of course, you treated Lydia wonderfully. How could you doubt it.'

'No.' Eduardo shook his head. 'I'm not sure I did. When she was packing up the house I hovered about —'

'As one does,' said Florence feelingly.

'— and I noticed most particularly that I had never written the word "love" on any of the Christmas or birthday cards I gave her. I watched her pack up — she'd kept everything, you know. Such a hoarder of memorabilia, Lydia always was. And I noticed for the very first time and to my great horror that for years I'd just written "To Lydia from Eduardo, Happy Christmas" or "Happy Birthday, Lydia — from Eddie." Never "love", I never wrote "love". I wish I had now. She'd kept all my cards, and never once had I written the word "love".

'Oh dear,' said Frederick.

'Perhaps,' said Florence tactfully, 'she knew you loved her and there was no need to write it.'

'And you're very reticent,' said Frederick, 'as we all know. Perhaps you had a whole world of love bottled up inside and were just too self-conscious to express it.'

'I wish I had now,' said Eduardo stubbornly. 'And if she arrives I won't be able to even tell her now because she won't be able to see me.' He put his face in his hands.

'We mustn't give in to depression,' said Frederick firmly, 'not after all we've been through. Eddie, even though you don't feel like it you must come with me down into the old sitting room — sadly it isn't the charming room you and I recall but we must do the best we can. Just come with me, Eddie, and strike a few chords, please. Lydia would have perfectly understood your absolute reticence in matters of the heart and she would have known you loved her. Why else would she have cried so terribly and for so long? Just think of it logically, Eddie. You used to say yourself that the sound of her weeping as she sat on these very stairs every night was so terrible you thought the birds might fall out of the sky.'

'I did,' said Eduardo. 'Yes, I see what you mean. Okay then — a little music. What harm would there be in it, after all.'

As Florence began to cast on the stitches for the collar of her cardigan she heard the initial notes of the fourth movement of one of Beethoven's piano trios. Slightly strange, she thought, with no cello. Quite an empty ghostly kind of sound really but, she thought comfortably, that was perhaps how it should be. Since Frederick had taught Eddie to sight-read Beethoven by the light of the moon on the nights the Crumlatchs went to the ladies' night dinner at the Rotary Club, things had gone better with the music. Then she sighed at the thought of all the ladies' nights they had had to endure, presaged by exactly the same little melodrama down in the entrance hall.

'You're not wearing that,' Kevin Crumlatch would say as Moira came down the stairs.

'What's the matter with it? I thought you liked this dress.'

'I might have quite liked it back in 1066 but we're now in the twenty-first century, Moira, in case you hadn't noticed. How do you think I feel when I have to take you out wearing what looks like a dishcloth?'

'If you gave me some money I could buy a decent dress.'

'If you had any brains you could run yourself up something on the sewing machine.'

Moira usually began to cry then. 'I haven't got a sewing machine.'

'What, Moira, would be the use of buying you a sewing machine when you can't even sew?'

After they had left Frederick and Eduardo would go down into the sitting room for a piano lesson. As she listened now Florence began to feel that Eddie had made real progress in the last few months. There was a delicacy about his touch, a fineness in his interpretation that showed a genuine ability.

'Bravo,' she called. 'Bravissimo, excell —' At this point she was dramatically interrupted as Claude came flying through the front door and hung, laughing a little wildly, from the bronze and glass light fitting in the hall. Its chain quivered slightly at the impact of his spectral presence. He was followed at a more sedate pace by Alexander McLeod who merely walked quietly through the front door and stood in the entrance hall with a small brown leather suitcase in one hand and his beige Braemac raincoat over the other arm.

'I'm terribly sorry,' he said apologetically, 'but I've come to stay for a while. No, that is a lie. I've come to stay permanently if you'll have me. Claude and I have discussed it overnight and he says I can share his room.' His voice took on a broken timbre. 'I just can't stand it down there any more — the loneliness, the isolation, the lack of any kindred spirit, it's just too awful. I can't take it any longer.'

Claude dropped to the floor from the light fitting and stared up at his astonished sister who had dropped her knitting again. The music had stopped and the house was almost completely silent.

'Florence,' said Claude, 'speak to me. Say something.'

'I'll work,' said Alexander McLeod, continuing desperately. 'Just say the word and I'll try anything. I can give you free medical advice, I can sweep and garden, I can haunt a place with the best. I can dangle and cackle and scream if you want me to. I can adapt to anything, only please, please let me stay. If I have to remain down there in my old surgery I'll go mad with loneliness. If I have to stay there a moment longer listening to that awful fellow who took over my practice putting me down all day long I'll kill myself.'

'So it's that bad.' Frederick was advancing, his hands outstretched. 'Welcome,' he said. 'If only we'd known about this earlier, Mr McLeod —'

'Please,' said Alexander McLeod, 'call me Alexander.'

'Alexander. If only we'd known. We had no idea things were so bad.'

Florence was bustling down the stairs, her knitting forgotten on the second landing. 'Of course you must stay,' she said. 'There's plenty of room here. And Frederick' — she gave her husband a sharp glance — 'we must try to make contact with your old friend, the one you were talking about earlier. He may be lonely too. Perhaps he might like to come to stay as well. We could have a kind of bed and breakfast place here.' Alexander McLeod put his suitcase down and patted his upper right-hand pocket where his chequebook used to be. 'No, no, no,' said Florence. 'That's not what I meant at all, Alexander. Everyone could stay free, of course, but we could just have everyone here.'

'Perhaps we might get enough musicians to have an orchestra,' said Frederick hopefully.

'I don't think so,' said Florence with uncharacteristic firmness, 'but perhaps we could manage enough musicians for a quartet or quintet.'

'Perhaps a small chamber orchestra?' Frederick had such an air of boyish hopefulness that Florence's heart was touched.

'Darling,' she said, 'if you want a chamber orchestra of course you may have one, but not all year round, please. Perhaps just in the summer months.'

'A summer music school,' shouted Frederick in a moment of inspiration. 'The place full of musicians for a few weeks during the best of the weather. Beethoven day and night. How marvellous. We may be able to make contact with the great man himself. What richness. What harmony. What joy.' He sank down on the bottom stair, murmuring faintly then started up again. 'How dreadful of me,' he said. 'How very remiss. Mr McLeod, I mean Alexander, none of us has asked what exactly was the matter with Claude who' — and he looked piercingly and humorously over the top of his glasses at Claude who was swinging ecstatically from the hall light fitting again — 'seems to be restored to perfect health in less than twenty-four hours, little short of a miracle.'

'Claude, dear — do be careful,' said Florence mildly from her perch on the stairs. 'It's wonderful to see you so early and so unexpectedly, but I do want to concentrate on my knitting.'

'Marvellous, isn't it?' Alexander McLeod regarded Claude with great satisfaction. 'But there's no great secret to it. All he needed, really, was intensive rest. There was nothing fundamentally wrong with his actual physical frame, as it were, if he had one.'

'I see,' said Frederick who was completely mystified.

'But I gave him some intensive therapy in my old heat room, now sadly removed by that clot Chun who's taken over my practice. And thorough examination of his humerus on the injured side showed that there was nothing seriously wrong there. The glenoid socket was in absolutely perfect condition —'

'Would you like a cup of tea?' said Florence desperately.

'— although I had at first suspected there may be something slightly awry there due to the impact with the other party.' Alexander put his small suitcase down on the floor of the entrance hall where it rested, glowing slightly, a few centimetres above the surface of the Crumlatchs' red nylon carpet. 'Furthermore the clavicle itself was also in perfect condition so I decided, after a full investigation, that the whole problem was caused by a simple inflammation of the rotator cuff muscles. The scapula was also absolutely topnotch.'

There was a long silence.

'My word,' said Frederick vaguely.

'And a biscuit,' said Florence.

'I beg your pardon?' Alexander McLeod seemed non-plussed.

'Would you like a cup of tea and a biscuit?' said Florence patiently. 'After your journey from town, Mr McLeod, I mean Alexander.'

'I see,' he said. 'Yes, that'd be very nice, thank you. Milk and no sugar.'

'Alexander and I went to a takeaway bar and got chips,' said Claude pertly. 'I've never had chips before. We also went walking round the streets, just when the shops were closing for the night, and I saw real surfboards in the window of a sports shop and golf clubs with metal shafts —'

'Claude dear, you're going to choke with excitement if you talk so quickly while you're hanging up there. I feel sure the human body just can't stand such strain, and please remember you have been ill,' said Florence. 'Do just drop down to the floor, there's a good boy, and come quietly out to the kitchen and tell me all about it.'

Alexander and Frederick heard his voice fading away towards the back of the house. 'And I looked in the window of a little shop in a side street that had a sign saying it was for adults only and saw these black transparent —'

'Thank you, Claude,' said Florence crisply — she could often be quite crisp — 'I think I've got the general idea.'

'But there were no girls,' said Claude sadly. 'There were no girls anywhere. I'd have really loved to see a girl. There might have been some inside the shop for adults. I could hear laughing and music and the sound of girls' voices but —'

They were never to know what stopped Claude from going inside because from the upstairs gallery, where Eduardo had desperately positioned himself much earlier because it gave an unparalleled view of the road, came a glad cry. 'The bus, the bus. The bus has arrived.' They had never heard such joy, such happiness, in Eduardo's voice. 'The bus, the bus.'

'Before anyone goes outside I've got something to confess.' Alexander McLeod stood at the foot of the stairs, blocking the way through the entrance hall. Behind him lay the enticing front door and they could hear voices and laughter and glimpse a flurry of movement beyond the trees that lined the drive to the house. 'I have some news to break to you,' said Alexander, who looked slightly wildly and hopefully in Claude's direction, 'unless you think, Claude, it might seem better coming from you?'

'No,' said Claude who was back dangling now thoughtfully from the light fitting, 'it's your news so I think you'll have to tell them.'

'What's his news?' asked Florence, who was packing her knitting away. 'What are you both talking about? Couldn't it be left till later on, till we've gone to see the bus? Frederick? Have a look through the glasses, dear, and see if you can see Lydia. I simply cannot believe —'

She was interrupted at this point by Alexander who spoke in a desperate tone. 'I've brought Timmy with me,' he said. 'I just couldn't leave him behind. We've been together so long. He's part of my life. In all my time down in the old surgery he's been almost my only companion. I couldn't leave him behind.'

'Timmy?' Frederick stepped forward. 'Your cat? Well, that's all right then. There's no problem with that, is there Florence my dear?' They both smiled blandly at Alexander McLeod 'Now do let us go by, Alexander — we've just got to see if Lydia's on the bus.'

'You don't understand.' If anything Alexander's expression became even more desperate. He gazed at Claude, perhaps for support.

'You've got to tell them,' said Claude. 'If they open the front door without knowing what's there it could be too much of a shock. And the lenses of the spectral spectacles may shatter with the accumulated atmosphere of emotional trauma.'

'A shock?' said Florence. 'Emotional trauma? What's outside the front door? I've seen hundreds of cats in my time. There'd be nothing about a cat —'

'Timmy is a horse.' Alexander McLeod spoke in a strangled voice, choked with emotion. 'Timmy's my horse. His full name is Kenilworth Osborn Wilmington the Fourth by Hydroxide out of Willowmede Grand Louise.'

'I beg your pardon?' Frederick stepped forward. 'No,' he said, 'don't say it all again, Alexander. This isn't by chance that racehorse you had years ago? That one who won the Golden Guineas and the Great Northern Steeplechase twice? The wonderful chestnut with the white blaze down his face?'

'Yes,' said Alexander more happily. 'that's Timmy. I always called him Timmy. I've kept him for years, since the terrible day he fell at the fifth fence the third time we thought we'd race him in the Great Northern. What a terrible day that was. My heart broke when I heard the rifle shot and knew that my Timmy was gone. Hopeless, hopeless,' he said. 'The fetlock broken. Nothing could be done at that time. Veterinary practises are different now, of course. Perhaps today my darling Timmy could be saved, but not then. I went home in a frightful state and it was only after I became a ghost myself somewhat later that I realised Timmy's indomitable spirit had returned to me. I cannot part with my Timmy. Timmy goes where I go. Wherever I go my Timmy comes with me.' He gave his chest a smart blow with his clenched left fist and stood like a Roman gladiator valiantly awaiting his lack of future.

Florence gave a sob and wiped her eyes with her lace handkerchief. 'What a beautiful story,' she said. 'Of course Timmy may stay. Where is he? We must go and see him immediately.'

'We tethered him to the birdbath,' said Claude, dropping lithely from the light fitting. 'I'm quite all right, Florence,' he said in an aside to his sister when she paled slightly at this. 'Alexander's fixed me up wonderfully. My shoulder's just fine and I won't have the same trouble ever again because I've been in his heat room and everything — don't worry, Florence. Just come outside and see Timmy.'

They gathered rather fearfully on the front portico but the horse was nuzzling happily on what was left of the lawn around the birdbath and raised his head to regard them with enormous brown eyes.

'He's very quiet,' said Alexander stepping forward gladly. 'There, there, Timmy, old fellow — nothing to be frightened of here. Just gather round quietly, everybody, and I'll introduce you all. Timmy,' he said proudly as he arranged the horse's glossy mane, 'was the means by which I was able to bring Claude home a little earlier to you than expected. We rode home bareback to save you the trouble of coming down to collect Claude this evening. Timmy's wonderful in traffic. Nothing bothers him. His spiritual sense of the inevitability of human nature makes him treat car horns and the appalling noise of present-day traffic with extreme aplomb.'

'I see,' said Florence doubtfully but hopefully. 'I'm not quite sure what you mean, Alexander, but it does sound awfully good. You always had a wonderful way with words, as I recall.'

'Thank you,' said Alexander modestly.

'But what will he eat?' asked Frederick. 'We don't have a hay field or anything like that. In the old days we used to let the lawn grow a bit down the bottom of the garden and it might have been a good place for a horse but Kevin Crumlatch has scraped the entire garden down to the bone. I doubt if a rose even dares to flower here these days, let alone enough grass to feed a horse.'

'Not a problem,' said Claude. 'We brought up his old hay bucket. He just keeps eating the same hay over and over again. And Alexander's got his nosebag of oats tucked away somewhere in his suitcase. No need to worry about the food.' He watched Frederick closely and as a slight frown passed over his brother-in-law's countenance Claude cried, 'Please let me have a horse. If only I could just have a horse I'd be so much better. I'd never ask again to go surfing or out in the car. I promise I'd never nag about all that again, if only I could have the horse. Please, Frederick, let me have the horse.'

'Of course we'll keep the horse,' said Frederick in a kind and fatherly manner. 'There just seems to be such a lot happening here today suddenly. I went into a little daydream thinking about it all. Perhaps, Claude, the first thing you could do is ride Timmy over to Reuben Grimwade's place, possibly tomorrow, and get him to come here. I feel he's probably very lonely over there by himself, but don't let's come to any arrangement about all that yet. You can easily ride over there and double him back, Claude. Now we simply must go up the drive to the gate and see what's going on with the bus or Eddie will die of impatience, won't you, Eddie?'

'I will,' said Eduardo and began to run lightly towards the front of the property. 'Lydia, Lydia,' he cried. 'Lydia. I'm sorry I never wrote "love" on your birthday cards. I just forgot. I was busy. I wasn't thinking straight. Lydia, Lydia.'

'One thing about Timmy that not a lot of people know,' said Alexander, 'is that he can count.' He seemed undeterred by Eduardo's sudden disappearance.

'Count?' Frederick looked amazed. 'The horse can count?'

'Yes,' said Alexander stoutly. 'Just watch this.' He stood in front of the animal and said clearly, enunciating the words in a slightly exaggerated way, 'How many people have you met here today, Timmy?'

The horse waited for a moment or two before tapping its right hoof on the ground five times.

'Remarkable,' said Frederick. 'What did you think of that, Florence?'

Florence stepped up to the horse and patted its nose tentatively. She had never been so close to a horse before. 'Brilliant,' she said. Then, 'How old am I?' The horse began to tap the ground vigorously with its hoof.

'For heaven's sake, Florence,' said Frederick with rare impatience. 'You're eighty-three. We're going to be here all day. Command cancelled,' he said to the horse. 'Sorry. Come on, Florence. We must get up to the gate quickly. Lydia just might be there.' He took the spectral glasses out of his pocket and put them on. 'I can see her,' he said. 'Yes, she's there. I see her sitting on the bus resting her head against the window. She looks very wistful. I think we'd better go, though, Florence, and see for ourselves. I'm getting a kind of muddled view here. It looks as if a very tall tattooed woman draped in very brief animal skins is standing up but I feel sure this can't be true. And she's being followed by a shortish Italian-looking man talking on one of those telephones without a proper cord. Come along, Florence. Take my arm, dear. Alexander? You must come too as you're part of the household now. Come along everybody.'

'Can I ride Timmy?' asked Alexander.

'Of course,' said Florence, 'if you want to.'

So they went through the trees of the old garden like a brilliant little invisible cavalcade, Alexander leading the way on Timmy who snorted proudly and tossed his mane, Claude running along beside the horse and its rider laughing happily, then Frederick following at a more sedate pace with his arm around Florence's shoulders.

Eduardo, far ahead, was waving to them as they approached. 'She's here, she's here,' he was shouting. 'I can see Lydia.'

'Oh Frederick,' said Florence, wiping her eyes with her lace handkerchief again, 'what a happy, happy day.'

CHAPTER
ELEVEN

So here we have the grand finale, like in a mediaeval play for villagers, when all the characters come on stage at the end to dance gladly and, in rhyming asides to the audience, reassure everyone that the story will turn out excellently. All the tangled threads will suddenly be embroidered meaningfully into a sweet pattern and all tears will turn to laughter, or at least to very hopeful smiles. Bent heads will lift, sad thoughts will become happy, invitations will be accepted, telephones answered, suitors who were turned away the first time will be looked at again and found acceptable, beds will be occupied by people who sleep tranquilly or make love deliciously and sincerely. That is how it will be. First, Lydia.

When the bus finally drew to a halt she stepped hesitantly off its lowest step, hardly daring to look at her old house. It seemed the same as when she left it a decade earlier, and yet curiously different. The drive, which had been gravelled, was now paved in red bricks hammered into place in a bed of the most coarse and unyielding grit laid upon industrial black plastic to stop the growth of weeds.

The magnolias that had once swept the ground with their far-flung branches were now trimmed back and presented stiff stumps up to above head height and after that the boughs poked stiffly out as if drawn there by a neat child with a thick black pencil. There had been no flowers on the trees because such a greenwood blooms on old timber and this had been dedicatedly trimmed away. The moss that had once crept up the old stones of the house's ground floor had been blasted away by high-pressure water treatments followed by acid applications so, austerely bleached, the house glared through the remnants of trees almost accusingly. It looked like an old lady caught naked in the bathroom, the flesh and the weaknesses exposed but the dignity forever caught at by arthritic but determined hands. Do not look at me how I am now — I was once beautiful. Lydia, standing at the gate, found the view both saddening and horrifying. Suddenly she was horribly aware of her discreetly tattooed thighs, the spoliation of herself by the stockbroker, the fishy feel of the semen of men whose names she did not even remember, the ring of the cash register, her expense account arranged by the Côte d'Azur for cosmetics, French perfume and silk underwear at the same department store Mrs Jackson went to on her days off for afternoon tea, the lies she had told . . .

The lies had been innocent enough within the framework of the life she had allowed to evolve — 'You were wonderful, darling,' to Mr Somerset-Smith, for example. And was this, in fact, a lie? Mr Somerset-Smith was an old man of exceptional courtesy, so was it a lie when she bent down to say through the taxi window, while delicately taking the extra tip that Mr Villetto knew nothing about, 'You were wonderful, darling'? Was that a lie? And was it a lie when she lay in the tangles of the best French linen sheets pretending that the men with her were Eduardo because that was the only way of getting through the evening and the night and the day after that and endlessly on forever?

Was it wrong to have wanted something better for herself, to have declined proposals of marriage from men she had thought were not a patch on Eduardo, and to have set off for the city thinking she might have another life, a different life and perhaps a better one? And when it all went wrong and she ended up as a cleaning lady for a rude and superior vicar — and there is no one more quietly rude than a superior vicar — and went out to dinner with the stockbroker she had once known vaguely when Eduardo was alive and the whole evening and her whole life turned to shit, was that a bad thing? What was a truth and what was a lie?

Perplexed, she stood at what had once been her old gate and said nothing. Her chiffon nightdress stirred faintly in the breeze and from far away she heard the call of seabirds on the shore. With a delicate sort of gaiety tinged with melancholy, she stepped daintily forward, pointing her bare toes. From one of them glimmered the large diamond solitaire given to her one Christmas by Charles Somerset-Smith.

Eduardo meanwhile had reached the gate and vaulted over. He stood next to her and took her hand in his.

'I think I can smell the scent of violets,' said Lydia, 'and yet there seem to be none growing under the trees as there used to be.'

'There now,' said gentle Florence, wiping her eyes again. 'Eddie will be happy now he's seen her.'

'Indeed,' said Frederick in a slightly choked voice. He, too, got out his best handkerchief, the one he always kept in the pocket of his dinner jacket, and wiped his eyes. 'The wind from the sea always makes my eyes water,' he said.

'Of course,' said Florence and then, brightening, 'Isn't it marvellous, Frederick, that we don't have to get afternoon tea or lunch for all these people? We're so lucky we aren't real any more, aren't we, dear? By the time I died I was so sick of cooking it nearly killed me. Just imagine serving homemade fresh scones with raspberry jam and whipped cream to all these people, and you'd need a savoury as well and perhaps a Victoria sponge. Imagine the work. And if we had to do lunch the very least we could serve would be various cold meats and two or three salads. The whole idea of it makes me shudder. Who do you think they all are, anyway? Is Lydia an actress now, do you think? Perhaps it's a group of theatrical people' — Samsonette was getting down off the bus now and was doing arm lifts just for a joke, with Alice dangling from her wrists — 'and look, darling, there's someone in a leopard-skin costume. Perhaps it's a circus? Is Lydia in a circus, Frederick?'

'Possibly,' said Frederick austerely in a slightly secretive manner. Of all things, he thought, gentle little Florence must never become acquainted with his sudden suspicions about the party from the bus at the gate. He had, during the First World War, been stationed in Paris for several weeks and there were certain aspects of the assembled throng that reminded him vividly of what he had seen there at the Folies Bergère. He looked around surreptitiously for ostrich feathers and anyone doing high kicks but, he thought, maybe they had left the more extravagant parts of their costumes behind, and possibly only did the high kicks at night. A rather well-tailored elderly man was wandering about with a splendid broom which he was using to dust the bus. Well, thought Frederick, times change and ideas of luxury change with them, but a broom? He looked at Oswald pensively.

'Isn't it wonderful to see her?' Eddie had joined them at the edge of the crowd. 'But she looks so —' He paused for a few moments. Oh heavens, thought Frederick, don't say poor Eddie's tumbled to what's been going on. 'So world-weary,' he said at last in a quiet sad voice. 'So irrevocably melancholy right into her bones.'

'Maybe she's just a little cold,' said Frederick hurriedly. What a pain in the neck it was being the oldest, he thought, and therefore in receipt of a greater knowledge of the frailties of the world. 'Perhaps she got a little chilled in the bus on the way here. People do get cold sitting still for any length of time. Perhaps it could be a good idea if you manufactured some kind of cosmic warmth around her, Eddie. She may get some colour back into those pale cheeks then.'

'Fabulous,' said Eduardo happily. 'I've already managed to make her imagine she can smell the scent of violets. I seem to be getting better at being a ghost, don't I? One day I might be as good as Claude.'

'Ha ha ha,' shouted Claude from his perch on Timmy's back. He had vaulted up behind Alexander and they were walking the horse carefully through the crowd. 'You'd have your work cut out to be as good as I am at dangling from light fittings.' He stopped suddenly when he saw Celine stepping off the bus. 'What a fabulous girl,' he said. 'Look at those legs. I must go and read what's written on her —'

'Thank you, Claude,' said Florence admonishingly as Timmy, spurred on, galloped nimbly through the crowd with Claude and Alexander, laughing wildly, on his back. 'That will be enough.'

Second, Richard Villetto and let's leave Lydia for the moment.

The cellphone began to ring vigorously in Richard Villetto's attaché case the moment they had all got off the bus. 'Yes, my sweetness and light?' he said wearily into the receiver. It would be Ambrosia again with some difficulty or another, possibly to do with catering. 'Yes, my dearest treasure and beloved only one, we have arrived safely.' There was a long pause in which he rolled his eyes heavenwards several times. 'I know, my darling,' he said, 'it's very difficult to give so many parties — so tiring for you. And I do agree you need a holiday. The exhaustion must be frightful, my own darling one. Yes, yes — Singapore if you like. You don't want to go to Singapore?' he murmured faintly after a few more minutes from Ambrosia. 'You want to go to Paris? Just wait one moment, my Aphrodite. If only I could bury myself in your —' He stopped there. 'My apologies, my little rose, my diamond, my little forget-me-not, I forgot for just one moment, for the merest moment in time — so do forgive me — that I never speak of our private moments in public. Of course you may go to Paris, my own beloved one, for your bridge tournament with your best friend Janetta Bumstead. Just wait one moment.' He got out his pocket calculator and did a some rapid arithmetic. 'All I need to do is increase charges over all by 7.2 per cent and overcharge dramatically on the liquor bills for politicians who never peruse the bill and can't do arithmetic anyway and you can stay in Paris for a fortnight at least, my beloved nymphet.'

He put the aerial down and placed the cellphone in his pocket. Thank heavens that was Ambrosia taken care of for a while.

Third, Mrs Jackson.

'I must say,' said Mrs Jackson to Oswald, 'I've enjoyed not having to make sandwiches. Although my life has many fascinating moments, I do get rather tired of making sandwiches.'

'Sandwiches?' said Oswald absentmindedly. He was looking up the brashly paved driveway: even Kevin Crumlatch's cruel hand on the pruning shears and the lawnmower could not dim the beauty of the scene before him. 'If only I had a garden,' he said faintly. 'If only I could live in a place like this just think of what I could do.' He took a few faltering steps forward and brushed a spider's web from the gates, placing a fond hand upon the palings of the front fence. 'I suddenly realise,' he said as if speaking to himself, 'that I have missed out on a great deal in life. I've been imprisoned in the city all these years and I never knew — just think of it, Geraldine — I never knew that life existed beyond the motorway. It looks lovely here.'

'It does,' said Mrs Jackson. 'If only we had had different lives, Oswald.' She sighed regretfully.

'Indeed yes,' said Oswald. 'But' — and he brightened visibly — 'things haven't been that bad, Geraldine. We have had our moments.'

'Mrs Lillian Anstruther,' said Geraldine Jackson with a faint giggle.

'Judge Anstruther,' said Oswald with a merry twinkle in his blue eyes.

'The accountant's wife who had red hair and much else, Oswald.'

'My, my,' said Oswald playfully. 'How well you know all my secrets, my dear Geraldine. And what about all those dear old grandfathers whom you meet at little Sebastiano's school? What about them, Geraldine?'

'And what about the grandmothers?' said Mrs Jackson

archly. 'Yes, Oswald, you certainly know my secrets and I know yours.' In sudden alarm she pointed up into the sky 'Oswald, Oswald. Whatever is that?' She seemed to have suddenly forgotten their deliciously scandalous pasts.

'It seems to be a helicopter,' said Oswald, shading his eyes. 'And it's going to land on the lawn.'

'No,' said Geraldine Jackson in mock horror.

'Yes,' said Oswald. 'Definitely.'

The girls all clustered around to watch it land and Celine, always prone to become aggressive, shouted, 'If that's some customer wanting me then he can go right back home again and boil —'

'Thank you, Celine,' said Mrs Jackson deftly. 'I don't think we need to worry about that. As I understand it, the Armageddon Room is absolutely closed till further notice and the Pinkney Pelle Parlour has agreed to take all urgent cases with its skeleton staff. I've always thought the girls there were far too thin anyway. There's nothing for you to worry about, my dear. It just seems to be some kind of dark-suited man with a very pallid complexion and a white Yves St Laurent shirt and a silk Paisley tie of somewhat the wrong width for the later nuances of this fashion season.' Mrs Jackson could never be faulted on her exact and encyclopaedic knowledge of fashion details gleaned from reading British *Vogue* while the Italian dishwasher churned through its jet-propelled cycles and the dishwasher-proof Royal Worcester sandwich trays came out pristine ready for the next influx of customers. 'It isn't anyone I've seen around the Côte d'Azur.'

She stared intently as the helicopter landed and the man prepared to jump out. 'He looks like a lawyer to me,' she said austerely, 'and as you know I'm not fond of lawyers. I don't include dear Judge Anstruther in that blanket statement. He was not a lawyer, of course, in the latter stages of his career. He was a judge, and married too,' she sighed regretfully, 'but he could have got a divorce if he had really wanted to, I always thought.'

Oswald frowned. Geraldine always got so upset when Judge Anstruther was mentioned because he had been her one true love, among many. Meanwhile he flicked a few more spiders and caterpillars off the gates with his Provençal broom and some of the girls ran through one or two dance routines as they propped the placards against the back of the bus. What a nasty noisy place the dear old world was, he thought as two cars collided mysteriously in the middle of the road and juddered to a halt, amid broken glass, in the gutter on the opposite corner. Celine, wielding a large black felt-tip pen with a very wide nib, and was quickly running up a few more notices:

NEVER DIRTY — JUST DEPRAVED
SEX AND VIOLENCE BUT CLEAN AS A WHISTLE
DO WE LOOK DIRTY TO YOU, BUDDY BOY?
COME AND HAVE A CLOSE LOOK ($100)

As she propped the last one against the garden fence another truck swerved violently and mounted the kerb.

The dark-suited man had climbed out of the helicopter and was making his way laboriously across the lawn towards them, ducking his head to avoid the rotor blades. He seemed to be already deeply scarred from previous mysterious injuries. Carrying a briefcase, he limped forward.

'Do forgive me,' he called as he approached the group at the gate. 'My name is Gilbert Anstruther —'

'Oh no,' gasped Geraldine Jackson, 'Not dear Judge Anstruther's only nephew, a noted legal eagle who was once badly wounded by a mad bomber after a lurid divorce case? Does this mean —?' She crumpled to the ground in a deathly faint.

'Uncle's fine,' said the lawyer calmly. 'And Auntie Lillian's quite settled in her mind. Last time I saw her she was building a replica of Balmoral Castle out of ice cream sticks, but without the Queen Mother of course. She's never quite mastered the human form and there are always problems with the miniature clothes. No, no — I've come on other business. Is there' — and here he consulted a large folio he had under his arm — 'a Mrs Lydia Briggs present at this gathering?'

Lydia stepped forward, her diaphanous draperies fluttering faintly in the violet-scented breeze from the sea.

'Frederick,' said Florence, clasping her hands and smiling brilliantly, 'doesn't she look wonderful. Hardly a day older and very little touched by the passage of the years. And just look at Eddie.' Eduardo had also stepped forward and, holding Lydia's arm tenderly and invisibly, walked with her up to the lawyer.

'Oh Frederick,' said Florence again.

'I never thought I'd see the day,' said Frederick as happy tears crept down his face. 'Do you have a hanky, Florence? I seem to have lost mine. I suddenly seem to have another attack of hayfever.'

'So have I,' said Florence in a trembling voice.

'Mrs Briggs,' said Gilbert Anstruther, 'I must congratulate you. May I shake your hand? I have flown here especially as per the instructions in the last will and testament of my old and valued client, one Charles Rennie MacTavish Somerset-Smith who sadly succumbed to the Great Reaper yesterday during his afternoon nap.'

Several of the girls began to sob at this news and Lydia paled visibly.

'He was always such a lovely man,' she said in a faint voice.

'However,' said Gilbert Anstruther, 'I bring good news in that he has left his entire estate to you, Mrs Briggs.' He consulted the papers from the folio again. '"Like a daughter", he says here. You are his sole legatee and executrix and, according to the terms of the will, I was to contact you at once and this I have done — by helicopter. I thought you'd want to know immediately.'

'Of course, of course,' said Lydia in an abstracted voice.

'Do you mean to say Mr Somerset-Smith has left me everything, even the house?' The lawyer nodded. 'My goodness me,' said Lydia.

'I don't think goodness had anything to do with it,' snapped Celine sourly but was silenced by a basilisk look from Geraldine Jackson.

'Congratulations, my dear,' she said, moving closer in her feather-trimmed mules, not entirely an easy task because of the uneven stonework on the drive and her very high heels. She clasped Lydia's hands. 'I hope you realise you're now a very wealthy woman,' she said. 'The world's your oyster.'

'Am I?' said Lydia. 'Is it?'

Eduardo clasped her arm firmly. She seemed so dazed, so helpless, so childlike and innocent. 'My treasure,' he murmured.

'If I've got so much money,' said Lydia, her voice stronger now, 'I'll buy my old house back. There seems to be a "For Sale" notice up by the front fence. If the people want to sell it then I'll buy it and we can have it as a holiday house for us, or a country branch, or a place where we can all retire to when we don't want to work any more.'

'Put me on the list,' called Oswald, 'and Geraldine wants to come as well.'

Lydia turned to the lawyer again in sudden embarrassment. 'That's if there's enough money,' she said apologetically. 'You must forgive me — I just got carried away for a moment.'

'Mrs Briggs,' said Gilbert Anstruther firmly, 'you could buy the whole street if you wanted to — and as for furnishings and so on, the contents of the house have been left to you lock, stock and barrel. Apart from the very minor legacy of a Sheraton bedroom suite and a sum of money for Charles Somerset-Smith's housekeeper to buy a small apartment with, the rest is yours entirely.' He eyed the big house through the denuded trees. 'I can tell you on very good authority that if you had a yen to hang a Monet or two in your stairwell you'd be very well able to, and plenty left over to sell at Sotheby's and satisfy the art world. And that's only the beginning.'

146

Later, when they all told their stories of that day, everyone's account was slightly different. Lydia said the sound of a police car's siren came after the lawyer's announcement. Celine, Samsonette and Mrs Jackson all said they heard it as the lawyer told her the news. The time of the arrival of the taxi containing Moira Crumlatch was also disputed. Oswald said it slid up to the gate at exactly the same moment as the police car. The younger girls and the three from the Pinkney Pelle claimed the taxi arrived first, closely followed by the police car, and that Moira Crumlatch climbed out of the car to say to the constable, 'Whatever are you doing here, officer? And who are all these dreadful people blocking my gateway?'

'Are you Mrs Moira Crumlatch?' said another police officer, stepping out of the car.

'I haven't done anything,' she said, 'have I? I've only been into town to see my lawyer. Officer, all I've ever had in my life is two parking tickets and they were years ago. Whatever have I done?' She began to cry. Most of the people gathered round the gateway of Lydia's old house were either crying, had been crying or were going to cry quite soon.

Even Oswald, not usually visibly prey to attacks of senti-ment, felt his eyes fill with tears when he heard the news about Charles Somerset-Smith and hid his embarrassment by wandering around the outside of the double-decker bus flicking off imaginary bits of dust with the Provençal broom.

Poor old Charles, he thought, even though he had never called Mr Somerset-Smith Charles in real life more than once or twice. Perhaps that housekeeper, Mrs Kirby, would already be packing things up and sealing drawers, cleaning out the refrigerator, drawing all the curtains and dealing with callers. She might even shed a tear or two herself as she regarded the small mute testimonies to Charles's diminishing needs and wants: perhaps the smallest size piece of Brie in the cheese compartment of the refrigerator, with only a tiny piece cut off it; a few of the better sort of crackers in an antique cake tin; more than half a bought Madeira cake left over from his

147

sparse afternoon teas. Oswald, feeling a reluctant tear creep down his cheek, put down his broom and leaned against the bus.

'Ossie dear,' said Geraldine Jackson, 'whatever are you doing here hiding behind the bus? And all covered with dust, too?' She began to brush him down. 'My poor old friend,' she said.

'He was indeed,' said Oswald.

'No, I mean you, silly,' said Mrs Jackson. 'Just stand still for a moment.' She brushed one side of his face lightly with her lace handkerchief. 'You must have a clean face for the TV cameras. Lydia's had good news and now someone else is getting bad news. Perhaps we could help somehow.'

'News?' faltered Oswald. 'More news?'

'Yes,' said Mrs Jackson, taking his arm. 'Come and hear the news.'

'I very much regret to inform you,' the policeman was saying to Moira Crumlatch, 'that there's bad news as far as you're concerned and, sadly —'

'Bad news,' echoed Moira. 'What kind of bad news? What do you mean, bad news?' Her voice was rising on a note of hysteria as the people from the bus, including Oswald and Mrs Jackson, clustered around.

'Perhaps we should go up to the house,' said the policeman, 'and some of these kind people' — Mrs Jackson and Oswald stepped forward — 'could make a cup of tea for you, Mrs Crumlatch.'

Geraldine and Oswald managed to rustle around in the kitchen of the old house amazingly well and in a very short time had put together a reasonably presentable tea tray, although they would later say how ashamed they had been of what they produced.

'Hardly a decent matching cup and saucer in the whole house,' Geraldine would falter as she bit her lower lip.

'And every biscuit in the place stale. Some even had mildew on them in the tins,' Oswald would aver stoutly. 'As for cake. As for a decent piece of cake — think again, Horatio. You'd be lucky!'

'But that's my best china,' murmured Moira Crumlatch when they handed her a cup of tea. Florence and Frederick, sitting on the stairs now in their usual perches, rolled their eyes ironically.

'Poor Moira,' Florence whispered softly. 'Kevin never even gave her a pretty teaset for her birthday, not ever in their married life. Now I remember, Frederick, you gave me so many that there was an entire section devoted to teasets in the catalogue of our estate auction. I do wish I'd gone to see them sold.'

'You might have been upset about who bought them,' said Frederick quickly, his eyes on what was happening in the sitting room with Moira Crumlatch and the policemen.

'I never use any of these cups and saucers,' Moira was saying hesitantly. 'They're for best.' Florence sighed again. By then Moira was slumped in a polyester velvet and foam rubber armchair. 'Of course,' she had been saying, 'we never really got on. In the beginning it wasn't so bad but we ended up poles apart and I'd actually gone into town to see my lawyer about a divorce — that's why I was out today. I'd gone to see the lawyer. What a shock, though, what a shock.'

'I'm sure it is,' said one of the policemen. 'It's always a dreadful shock, no matter what the circumstances. I feel sure, even though your marriage had possibly reached an end, you wouldn't have wanted your husband to pass away, but that, sadly, is what happened slightly earlier this morning. We have the industrial safety people coming in shortly to re-inspect the wiring at the shop but there was nothing whatever to suggest, up till now, that there was any difficulty with electricity in the building.'

You mean —?' faltered Moira.

'Exactly.' The policeman spoke softly and kindly. 'Please be assured, Mrs Crumlatch, that it was instantaneous. Your husband would have felt nothing. All he would have thought was that he was going to turn all the lights on at the main. He would have reached out for the switch and that would have been the last thing he knew.'

Claude gave Frederick a violent nudge. The ghosts had all clustered around Moira's chair. 'You don't think he'll come back here, do you,' whispered Claude urgently to Frederick, 'and want to live here with us?'

'Surely not,' murmured gentle little Florence, her face drawn with concern.

'If you all wait one moment,' said Frederick, 'I'll put the cosmic glasses on and see if I can get some news of him. Yes, I'm seeing him now. He's sitting in his office looking very dazed and shattered. I'm not sure the news has really sunk in yet but realisation will come by twilight.'

'As it always does,' said Florence softly.

Frederick twiddled a tiny knob on the side of the glasses and seemed to look intently through their lenses for at least a minute.

'Please hurry,' murmured Florence anxiously.

'I'm beginning to see a little bit into his mind,' said Frederick at last. 'I think he's realising there's been an accident and he's no longer part of the real world. He's noticing people can't see him and yet he's seen himself carried away in the ambulance. He's very puzzled, poor man, but he's deciding, I think, that he'll stay there in the shop.'

'Thank heavens.' Florence placed her hand on her brow. 'Just for a moment I was deeply afraid that —' She stopped there.

'Quite so,' said Frederick. 'You thought he might come back to the house, but he never liked the house. He always preferred the shop, or the Rotary Club. You know what it's like, my dear — we go where we've been most happy and if such a man could be said to be happy, it was when he was at his shop and his club and that's where he'll stay I feel sure.'

Meanwhile, Mrs Jackson was pouring Moira a second cup of tea while Oswald, having vainly tried to find some fresher biscuits, returned from the kitchen. 'My dear,' said Mrs Jackson as she handed Moira the cup, 'this has been a very lovely home in it's day, if I may say so. Legally speaking, you have quite an inheritance here.'

'Yes,' murmured Moira Crumlatch in a faint voice. 'I mean no. I don't know what I mean.' She reached out her work-worn hand and took a stale arrowroot biscuit. 'Usually Kevin only lets us have biscuits on Sundays but maybe I'd better have something sweet. I might need the sugar.'

'Hmph,' snorted Oswald now from his position beside the teapot. He was stirring the tea with a large spoon to make it stronger. 'The catering around here has got to alter,' he whispered to Geraldine Jackson, 'if we're going to stay here.'

'Are we going to stay?' whispered Geraldine.

'Definitely,' said Oswald stoutly. 'I feel it's time we retired and what better place would there be to live usefully than here, in Lydia's old home?'

'She might not want us,' said Mrs Jackson. 'Have you asked her?'

'No,' said Oswald, still stirring the tea in the teapot, 'but in a big place like this any help is like hen's teeth, my dear Geraldine. We would definitely be wanted to do dusting and odd bits of cleaning, a little reception work perhaps if Lydia sub-leases the place to Mr Villetto for an out-of-town branch, sandwich-making, etcetera.'

'How do you know all this?' asked Mrs Jackson in a mystified voice.

'I don't,' said Oswald, 'but it stands to reason, if you think about it. I mean, just take a peek at Richard Villetto as we speak, Geraldine. If that's not a look that's sizing the whole place up, then I'm a Dutchman.'

Richard Villetto, oblivious of everyone else, did seem to be pacing out the size of the rooms and doing calculations on his pocket calculator.

If you hold a pack of cards in your hand and flick through them, you get a flashing glimpse of them all, like the fragments of the story that day.

Frederick feels deeply troubled about Kevin Crumlatch's departure. 'Even though we didn't like the man,' he says reflectively as the moon rises on another untroubled summer night, 'we shouldn't really have wished him dead the way we did. I walked through him, you may recall. I mean, Florence, I do feel a sense of shameful chagrin about our all joining hands and willing him to have a heart attack.'

'No, no, darling,' Florence says patiently as she casts on the sleeve of her pink cardigan to start knitting it all over again. 'You've remembered it wrongly, my dearest one. We always meant to do that, but we never did. We just never got round to it, what with one thing and another.'

'Didn't we?' Frederick is a little bewildered, his white hair standing almost on end above his noble brow.

'Of course not, my sweetheart.' Florence gazes at him indulgently. 'We always meant to, but we didn't do it. No, no. It wasn't our fault. We meant to get rid of him, but we didn't: he met with a tragic accident and that was that.'

So that is one flick of the cards with one little picture, and flick, flick, here is the farmer in the Versace tracksuit standing beside his telephone in a large and echoing homestead set amid a grove of trees and with great lands sweeping down to the sea. With a photocopied card held carefully in his hand, he is dialling a number and waiting for an answer.

'Not there any more?' he says in a very disappointed voice. 'But I most particularly wanted to speak to her. Inherited a fortune? Retired from the business? Gone to live in the country? You can give me her number? How marvellous. And truly inherited a fortune you say? So you're not joking? Good gracious, what splendid news. Bought her beautiful old house back? Fantastic. Gone back to live in her old home town? Wonderful. Just let me get a pen and a piece of paper and I'll write down the details. Thank you so very much. I inherited a fortune myself,' he says absentmindedly as he writes. 'Odd how one can confide in someone one doesn't know, isn't it? My father left me this enormous place but it's rather lonely, really. One seldom meets anyone with whom one has such a sense of kinship.'

Flick, flick, the cards turning over now, the colours bright, the numbers mostly lucky. The telephone ringing in the old house, where the scene is one of disarray because the apricot polyester curtains have all been taken down and are in a pile on the floor. The windows open onto the dark night like a series of mysteries. Far away the sea glimmers under a rising moon. On the floor lie some enormous parcels that contain pale blue silk velvet curtains to be put up tomorrow. 'Hello?' says Lydia as she lifts the receiver. 'Who? I'm not at all sure I recall —' And she stops there. It is that farmer in the Versace tracksuit, she thinks, the one who offered to bring his white mare for her to ride. 'Of course,' she says. 'Yes indeed, I do remember now. How very kind of you to ring. Dinner? Tomorrow? Yes, that would be very nice, but' — and she pauses for a significant moment or two — 'are you possibly aware that —'

'Yes,' he says quickly. 'I am, yes.'

'Oh I see,' says Lydia. 'Mostly, in recent years, I haven't just gone out ordinarily to dinner, if you see what I mean.'

'Well,' says the farmer, 'I'd really like you to just come out ordinarily to dinner with me and afterwards I'll just take you home again. Maybe we could kind of get to know each other.'

'If it isn't too late,' said Lydia.

'It's supposed never to be too late,' said the farmer.

'I think it is sometimes,' said Lydia.

'Possibly, but we'll pretend it isn't.'

'If you're sure,' says Lydia.

'I am,' he says.

Flick, flick. There's Timmy tethered down in the garden and Claude, glad and carefree like a boy on holiday, riding him gently round the grounds every day. Alexander watches quietly from the upstairs windows, but there is not a lot of time for leisure because the ghosts are going through their music and preparing for a small private concert. The redecorations in the house have spurred the ghosts on to reorganise their own things and rethink their attitudes. Florence thinks she will be less reclusive and might walk into town more to look at the shops. Frederick has decided to take up his music again. Claude is less sulky because he has Timmy to ride and Alexander McLeod to talk to and there is so much going on in the house that it is a most stimulating environment. Apart from anything else, the vigorous and fruity repartee of the plumbers would enliven anyone for years. There is a lot of plumbing being done because extra bathrooms and cloakrooms are needed, even though this provincial branch of the Côte d'Azur will be very small and exclusive with no more than three customers per evening and operating only five nights a week.

Occasionally the rumble of a removal truck is heard in the drive and Lydia, looking younger and less citified than formerly and wearing camel-coloured velvet jeans with a tartan shirt and only one gold bangle, goes out to meet the drivers. 'Just put it all in here, please,' she says as the consignments of furniture are unloaded. The big Louis the Fifteenth gilded stool goes in front of the fireplace, the exact position it had in Mr Somerset-Smith's old house. The French gilded armchairs he and Oswald sat on the morning Mrs Kirby brought them tea and toast are placed strategically so that anyone sitting in them will get the best view down the valley to the sea. Eduardo often sits in one now, smiling happily, to watch Lydia go about her tasks. When he holds her hand she says the old house has become very warm and always has a scent of violets, though none grow now beneath the old windows. 'I must plant them again,' she says. Two of the Monets have been sent down under armed guard to hang on the stairs and beneath their gilded frames, illuminated by the glow from the waterlilies, Florence now sits contentedly most evenings knitting Frederick a pair of gloves. Later in the winter she will knit Alexander a jersey, then Reuben, but she does not know that yet.

Moira Crumlatch, dazed with the splendour, wanders about the house with a special yellow duster Lydia has purchased for her. On the day legalities were resolved Lydia bought the property on the understanding Moira could remain living in it forever. Mrs Jackson held her hand and said, 'You can help me with the sandwiches, my dear,' and Moira Crumlatch cried and said, 'I won't be lonely any more. This is the only place I've ever lived where I've felt I could reach my full potential as an individual.'

'Perhaps club sandwiches then,' said Geraldine, 'and maybe cut into fancy shapes with exotic garnishes.'

Richard Villetto had flown down from the city to sign his partnership deal with Lydia and was present for the Crumlatch signing just before his own contract was legally clinched. He looked at Moira assessingly and reflectively, noting her neat ankles and legs that were better than he had expected.

'See what you can do,' he whispered to Geraldine Jackson as he generously and discreetly handed her a sheaf of notes. 'Take her to a beauty salon,' he whispered, 'and clean her up a bit. Maybe she might bloom a little and we could use her on reception, do you think? Her eyes are a very pretty colour if you really look at them, but the problem is I don't think anyone ever has.'

'Leave it to me,' said Mrs Jackson serenely. 'I think a pale pinkish-brown lipstick,' she murmured to herself, 'with no blue tones.' Already she was happily redecorating Moira Crumlatch in her own mind.

The final flick of the cards comes when two small, but momentous events occur in a single day. The first is the sight of Mrs Huddlestone bicycling vigorously in the gate, waving what looks like an old-fashioned telegram in one hand. All news comes to the ghosts in a manner they will readily understand. When Frederick purloins a newspaper around the house and reads the finance pages they blur faintly and reassemble themselves as the columns were organised before computerisation came to the local rag and the management altered the typeface. In his hands, the newspaper becomes what Frederick fondly recalls. Faxes evolve into telegrams in the time it takes to draw a breath. All telephones are black. So here is Mrs Huddlestone cycling up the red paved drive waving a telegram.

'Dreadful news,' she shouts happily to Florence and Frederick who have seen her coming and are leaning out an upstairs window. 'My granddaughter has been in a train accident in North India — on her OE, of course. They will go away these days. When I was young we had to stay at home and work. But' — she flings her bicycle down on the lawn with unaccustomed carelessness and strides through the front door into the house — 'there isn't a mark on her by all accounts, and after —'

'Quite so,' says Frederick from the head of the stairs. 'We understand perfectly what you mean.'

'Well, anyway,' says Mrs Huddlestone slightly apologetically, 'she's coming to see me. She wants her old Gran,' she says proudly. 'It's been such a shock for her — she needs me. She's been asking for her Granny.' She delves around in her capacious handbag. 'Now here's her picture,' she says to Claude who has followed Frederick and Florence down the stairs. Oblivious to the spectral drama evolving in the entrance hall, Moira Crumlatch is still flicking around with a duster and Lydia, meanwhile, is talking on the telephone to Richard Villetto.

'No, I don't think I'll really work again, Richard,' she is saying. 'I'll just live here quietly and kind of act as manageress, I think, and Geraldine and Oswald can help out when I'm away sometimes. Away? Yes? Didn't I tell you. I'm going to be away sometimes staying on a farm. How are things up your way, anyway? Oh good. No, I don't think I'll ever come back to the city. I think I'll just stay here and be happy. All that French furniture looks stunning here and as for the Monets — well, need one say more than that, Rickie?'

'She's a really lovely girl,' Mrs Huddlestone is saying to Claude who gazes, enraptured, at the photograph of Mrs Huddlestone's granddaughter. 'As soon as she arrives to stay with me I'll bring her over and introduce you to her. She might be arriving next Wednesday. Certainly by the end of next week she'll be here.' Within moments of all that, a quiet figure comes in the front gate. Yet another visitor approaches the house and rings the doorbell.

'Why don't they answer it,' says Florence quite crossly to Frederick. 'That doorbell ringing and ringing like that is getting on my nerves.'

'Aha,' says Frederick, rising from his seat on the stairs. 'It may be for us, my dear. Perhaps' — and he nods towards Lydia and Moira — 'the ringing of the doorbell is suddenly beyond their ken.' He strides past Moira and Lydia and opens the door. 'Do you remember me?' says a man with a small valise in one hand and a violin case in the other who is loitering disconsolately in the portico. 'I'm so lonely I can't stand it any more. I've packed all my things and come over.'

'It's Reuben,' cries Frederick gladly. 'Reuben — how marvellous. We can have a trio now. Alexander's here, but I'll explain all that later. We were going to send Claude over one night to get you but what with one thing and another we hadn't quite got round to it. There's been such excitement here. Do come in,' he says, 'and take no notice of all the mess everywhere. Lydia's back and she's restoring the old house to what it was. Just step around those parcels of curtains and watch out for the plumbers. They're apt to pop up when you're least expecting them. Welcome, welcome,' he says. 'You can stay forever. Things are going to be much better around here from now on. You're just in time for all the fun.'